R0084215482

07/2016

When You Step

DISCARDED:

OUTDATED, REDUNDANT
MATERIAL

D1366836

PALM BEACH COUNTY
LIBRARY SYSTEM
3650 Summit Boulevard
West Palm Beach, FL 33406-4198

When You Step

J. E. HARRIS

A NOVEL

two harbors press | *minneapolis, mn*

Copyright © 2016 by J. E. Harris

Two Harbors Press
322 First Avenue N, 5th floor
Minneapolis, MN 55401
612.455.2293
www.TwoHarborsPress.com

All rights reserved. No part of this publication may be reproduced,
stored in a retrieval system, or transmitted, in any form or by any means,
electronic, mechanical, photocopying, recording, or otherwise, without
the prior written permission of the author.

This book is a work of fiction. It is not meant to portray, represent, or
depict any real person. All names, characters, dialogue, and incidents
are either products of the author's imagination or are used fictitiously.
Any resemblance to actual events or persons, living or dead, is entirely
coincidental.

ISBN-13: 978-1-63413-939-7
LCCN: 2015921063

Distributed by Itasca Books

Cover Design by Lois Stanfield
Typeset by E. Keenan
Author Photo by T.P. Photography, Minneapolis, MN

Printed in the United States of America

✦ *Dedication*

To the GIRLS who give me purpose.
To the MAN who gives me balance.
To the STEPPERS who gave me a story.

✑ Acknowledgments

I must first thank God for granting me a sound mind and the ability to put words to paper.

I thank my beautiful, smart, and funny daughters, Jessica Grace and Jayna Isabel, for their critiques and commentary, both solicited and not. I love you both to the moon and back.

As for my favorite stepping instructor, Dwight, thank you for having faith and confidence in me when I did not, and encouraging me to "just write it!" You *are* my one and only.

Essential shout-outs to each of the phenomenal women in my life: Ella, DeAnn, Dawn, Kirstin, Ruby, Jackie, Kim, Tasha, Val, Phyllis, Vandella, Jeaneane, Sondra, Heidi, and Theresa. Thank you for being that brilliant, wonderfully diverse, animated, vibrant, and entertaining group that has provided the collective inspiration only for the most delightful characters in this story. You all bring joy to my world and I am so blessed to have you in it.

Thank you to the oh-so-talented renowned artist, Synthia Saint James, who was gracious and kind enough to read my book and offer her congratulations and praise.

Thank you to Markie Bee, editor extraordinaire, who took time out of his busy schedule to share priceless words of wisdom.

Last, but certainly not least, a loud Delta Sigma Theta thank you to my Omega Psi Phi brother, Marty Majeske, who put his valuable artistic stamp of approval on my first endeavor as a writer.

Finally, I would like to recognize the expertise and professionalism that has been afforded to me by my publisher, Two Harbors Press. The staff and leadership truly care about your final product, whether you are an established author or new to the game. Anyone who knows me, knows that I am a bit of a perfectionist. They handled it like the champs that they are and I would definitely repeat the experience…(hint).

On that note, thanks in advance to all who have read and will read my book. It has truly been a good time, and I hope that fact shines through on the page.

"When you dance, your purpose is not to get to a certain place on the floor. It's to enjoy each step along the way."

—Wayne Dyer

∞ *Chapter One*

"You aren't wearing *those* shoes with that dress, are you, Mom?" Grace asked in her usual critical tone.

"What's wrong with my shoes, Grace?" I asked.

"The same thing that's always wrong with your shoes, Mom. I'm going to get the silver ones."

"Hey, I think Mom looks pretty," Isabel jumped in.

"Thank you, Isabel. You know Grace always has to find something wrong with what I'm wearing."

"She's just trying to suck up because she wants to go to the movies," Isabel whispered. "I like the shoes Mom has on, Grace. And did you ask her yet about going on your date?"

"Shut up, Isabel!" Grace snarled. "And what do you know about dresses and heels anyway? You wear jeans and sneakers every single day!"

"Maybe so, but I still look better than you in those lacey, ruffled, crazy—"

"Okay, okay. Enough," I interrupted. "Let me try the silver shoes, Gracie."

"OMG, much better, Mom." Grace nodded with a big smile of approval.

"You look beautiful, Mom." Isabel smiled even wider.

"Beau-ti-ful. Guys will be waiting in line to dance with you all night," Grace complimented, definitely about to ask for something. "Want me to grab your silver clutch to match your shoes?"

"What do you want, Grace?"

"I told you she wants you to let her go to the movies with her *boyfriend*," Isabel said, tattling again.

"Shut up, Isabel. You suck!" Grace screamed.

"You suck too!" Isabel retaliated.

"Both of you be quiet," I ordered. "Grace, have you asked your dad about this movie?"

Grace replied with a defeated, "Never mind."

"Anyway, have fun tonight, Mom. Even though I tease you, you are the most beautiful woman I know, inside and out," Grace said with some sincerity. "And besides, you should follow your own advice to us. You always tell us 'if you carry yourself in the right way and treat everyone with respect, the same treatment will be returned to you,'" Grace mocked me in her best *mom* voice. "Guess you were wrong."

They both giggled.

"You know what, Grace, that is absolutely correct, *most* of the time," I reassured her, "but sometimes . . ."

"Okay, Mom," Grace said dismissively. "Have fun anyway . . . tell Auntie Stacey and Miss Vivian we said 'hi.'"

"Both of you in bed by eleven thirty. I love you."

"Love you too," they replied in sync.

∽

My name is Gabrielle Grant, but most of my friends call me Gigi. I am a forty-something single mom of two beautiful daughters. My girls always had a way of knowing how to push my buttons, mostly by throwing my own words back in my face. Grace, my sixteen-year-old self-proclaimed fashionista and mini-me-actress-wannabe, is the girliest girl I know. She would wear a twirly dress every day if she could. She spends much of her day talking about boys and acting and dances and shopping and friends. Her little sister, Isabel, my almost fourteen-year-old, is interested mostly in making life miserable for Grace. She heckles and teases and steals Grace's cell phone, all while trying out for every sports team there is. Though, at the end of the day, they would not know what to do without one another. They may not know it yet, but they are definitely best friends.

As for me, it took about twenty years to realize that I needed to enjoy life by living it for myself instead of someone else. I was a baby bride and really didn't know how to do anything but love someone else, and it turned out that I was no expert at that either. After ten years of marriage, I found myself divorced at the ripe old age of thirty, raising two babies on my own. Don't misunderstand, my girls are my pride and joy, and I have created quite an impressive interior decorating reputation for myself to make sure that they have everything that they need and some things that they want. For the past ten years, most of my life has been spent working, cooking, cleaning, and chauffeuring—you know, the regular mom duties. I always spent about a week each summer following my daughters around various amusement parks and calling it a vacation. And then another week having fun with my grown-up girlfriends, too—jazz festivals, weekends in Miami, LA, and New York City, exotic island vacations with lots of young, hot . . . you get the idea. Adventures, indeed. But I must admit that nothing I had experienced so far could have prepared me for the entirely unexpected and unbelievably dramatic journey I began a little over a year ago.

∽

"C'mon, Gigi," pleaded Vivian, "you said you would come to class with me!"

"I don't know, Viv. I'm not sure I have the time," I answered, motioning the girls to get into the car.

"You know we are a few months into a new school year. Grace has all of those play rehearsals, projects, and performances, and Isabel is in every sport imaginable. And the holidays are right around the corner! I'm always running behind the girls, getting them where they need to be. Once I get home, make dinner, do homework, and am finally able to have a seat, the last thing I am thinking about is dancing."

"All the more reason you should come to class," reasoned Vivian. "The girls are getting older, and you have sitters you trust to check in on them when you're not there. You could use a few hours away once a week . . . and a new class just started right down the street! How long have you been talking to me about learning how to step?"

"Ugh . . . okay, okay. How much is it?" I asked, still looking for a way out.

"First class is free, Gigi. I will be looking for you on Thursday." She motioned with two fingers at her eyes.

"Damn, Viv. I'll be there," I said. "But not next week; after Thanksgiving."

"All right. Deal. By the way, I had to trim Grace's hair today. Split ends."

"Thanks, Viv. It looks fabulous as always," I smiled.

Vivian Monroe was that one-of-a-kind friend who was exactly as she appeared, regardless of the circumstances. You know the type. She said out loud what everyone else was only thinking. She made fun of people right in front of their faces. And she always, always knew something about absolutely everyone.

I met Viv a little over eight years ago, not long after my divorce. One Saturday morning I arrived at my hair salon only to discover that my stylist had called in sick that day. Viv had been elected to deliver the news to me, but she was also happy to step in and take care of my hair that morning. The rest is history. As my daughters grew older, Viv started caring for their hair as well, from braids to straightening. About a year after my first "Vivian Original," she had saved enough money and had grown a large enough client base to open her own hair and makeup salon.

Over the years, I learned that Viv was also a single mom doing all that she could to make life better for her two children. Her kids were a little older than mine, but we had had some real conversations about what it meant to essentially be alone in this world as a single Black woman, doing what you had to do to survive. She was resilient and persistent and was friendly to everyone. At least until you insulted her intelligence. Viv was definitely one of those chicks to whom the phrase "you can't tell a book by its cover" most definitely applies. When I met her, I thought her blouse was too low cut, her shorts were too short, and her heels were too high. Now we go shopping together.

∽

"Stacey, guess who is going to class next Thursday?" I asked my friend in an exasperated tone.

"What? I can't believe it! I have been begging you to go to class for more than a year, sis. What made you change your mind?" Stacey asked.

"Well, I was picking up the girls from Vivian and . . . "

"She finally got to you!" Stacey was hysterical with laughter at this point. "I told Viv if we ganged up on you, we would get you there. I am going to have to offer her proper congratulations when I see her next Saturday for my appointment."

"Will you be in class next week?"

"Not next week, honey. I have a board meeting for one of my charities. I will be sure to tell CJ and Cameron to take care of you, though."

"Okay, Stace, what's really up with this stepping thing? Give me the scoop."

"Girl, don't believe everything you hear. You know that in any situation where you are bringing the opposite sexes together, there can be drama, but keep your wits about you and learn the dance. My only piece of advice is to be friendly enough to make business connections because you never know. How are my goddaughters?"

"The girls are fine, but they haven't seen Auntie Spoil Them Rotten in a while," I teased.

"I know, I know. I will be sure to see them on Thanksgiving. Is Monty coming to town?"

"Yes, ma'am, Monty will be here on Thanksgiving and staying for a week."

"Excellent. We will have to carve out some time so that Greg and I can meet you guys for dinner."

"Sounds like a plan, sis."

"Okay. Gotta run, but we will talk soon. Call me after your first class!"

I first met Anastasia Andrews, or Stacey as most people called her, when we pledged the graduate chapter of the same sorority almost twenty years ago. Since then, she has been one of my nearest and dearest friends, like a sister to me and an aunt to my girls. Stacey was a successful publicist to several local celebrities; but her real passion was doing charity work for nonprofits. Now that I think about it, it must be going on four years ago now since she told me she met her stepping instructor while serving on the board of one of her charities. Stacey was the kind of woman who always maintained her professionalism at all costs. Her husband of eight years, Gregory, was an attorney by day and an elected local government official in his spare time. They had two children and one perfectly groomed springer spaniel.

Stacey moved to Charlotte, North Carolina, about two years ago when Greg had an opportunity to head up a new law firm in the area. When the partnership failed, they moved back to Minneapolis after only a year, and she had been inviting me to join her in stepping class ever since. When she finally coaxed Vivian into joining last summer, they made it their mission to pull me in next. The interesting thing about Stacey was that she approached stepping the same as she approached most things in life—as a potential business opportunity. She enjoyed the dance and was quite good at it after four years, but her goal was to develop business relationships within the circle. You see, most of the steppers, at least in Stacey's circle, were entrepreneurs of sorts. Whether they were aspiring artists or musicians, owners of clothing and apparel boutiques, carpenters, or masters of some other skill, self-employment appeared to be all the rage.

When Stacey was searching for a new stylist, I introduced her to Vivian and they became friendly. Although they had known each other for close to five years, the two of them never went out without me tagging along. I truly believed it was always a positive experience to be exposed to different walks of life. And when it came to the spectrum of differences, Vivian and Stacey were on directly opposite ends.

∽

"Hey, baby," Monty greeted. "Been trying to call you for the last few hours. Where've you been?"

"I was picking up the girls from Vivian," I answered. "Do you know she and Stacey have finally talked me into going to a stepping class?"

"What? Are you really gonna do it?" Monty asked.

"I told them both I would check it out," I said.

"You know I don't think I can get used to the idea of other men with their hands on my lady."

"Whatever, Monty. Can't wait to see you," I responded, quickly changing the subject.

"Oh yeah! Can't wait, baby. Missing every inch of you."

"Miss you too."

Montgomery Lewis was my "boyfriend." I had really struggled with that word since I reached the age of forty and all, well most, of the men I had dated over that last few years had been over the age of forty-five. Hardly boys. I met Monty at a party Stacey and her husband hosted about nine months ago. He asked me to marry him after knowing me for about three hours. Can anyone say *red flag*? But there was something about him. Something wild and daring that allowed me to become a little wild and daring too.

Monty and I had a whirlwind romance. Beach vacations, cruises, and plans to go to Italy for a two-week holiday vacation. Even though it was a long-distance relationship, he was everything I needed in a man. You know the type, a real "man's man." He rode a motorcycle but collected classic cars, smoked cigars, and drank whiskey. He had a never-ending love of sports and an insatiable hunger for sex. In fact, if he could have sex while watching sports, he would be at his happiest. I suppose most men would share in that particular type of happiness.

Anyway, Monty was one of those guys who elicited an "Are you sure?" from your closest girlfriends who knew you best. "Are you sure he's your type?" "Are you sure he's right for you?" "Are you sure he will set a good example for your girls?" Monty definitely wasn't my usual type, the quiet, reserved businessmen I customarily dated—but he somehow made me believe that my *usual type* wasn't working—so I had to try something new and different. Monty was definitely something different.

∽

"Mom!" Grace yelled. "You said you wanted to be up by now to start dinner!"

"I'm up, I'm up," I lied.

"Isabel has already started peeling potatoes," Grace said.

"Okay, I'm coming." Even though the clock read 6:00 a.m., the late autumn sky said midnight. As I rubbed my eyes awake, I knew I needed to start moving because it was Thanksgiving morning. I could never get my kitchen to smell like my mom's did when I was growing up, but it was going to be a great day nonetheless. I was headed to the airport in a few hours to pick up Monty.

"Hey, Stacey!" I answered my phone with a smile.

"Hey, girl, letting you know that Greg just headed to the airport to pick up Monty."

"What?"

"Yep, I figured he hadn't told you. He called Greg a few minutes ago and asked him to grab him because he landed early. He mentioned that he knew you were in the middle of a big day and would surprise you."

"Well, what kind of surprise would that have been had I headed all the way to the airport to pick him up?" I replied, completely irritated at this point.

"I know, but you know how those two are. They go so far back it's like some kind of weird, unspoken brotherhood. Don't get upset with him before you even see him, G."

"I know, but sometimes . . . ugh! I haven't seen him in two months. I just wish he would have at least sent me a text to let me know. I would have given him and Greg their boy time. I'm sure they are headed off to watch some form of football at least three of the six nights he is here."

My phone buzzed with another call.

"Hold on, Stace. It's Vivian on the other line," I said.

"Happy Thanksgiving, Gigi!" Vivian said.

"Thanks," I answered. "You too."

"Damn, what's wrong with you?" Vivian asked. "Sounds like somebody stole your bike!"

"Hold on, let me add Stacey to our call."

"Hey, Stace, happy turkey day!" Vivian said.

"Thanks, honey," Stacey said. "Same to you."

"What the hell is wrong with Gigi?" Vivian asked.

"Monty just landed . . . and he didn't tell Gigi that he asked Greg to grab him from the airport, so she's a little bent out of shape," Stacey explained.

"What's new?" Vivian asked. "He's always doing that kind of thing, Gigi."

"Show a little empathy, Viv. Gigi hasn't seen him in a while."

"Hmm. Well, if you ask me—" Vivian started.

"I didn't!" I said.

We all laughed.

"It's all good. I know exactly who Monty is, so I am going to try to make a peaceful day of it," I said.

"Uh-huh," Vivian mumbled. "Stace, did Gigi tell you she's coming to class next week?"

"She sure did," Stacey said. "Nice work, Viv. I knew we would get her hooked if we waited long enough."

"You two go ahead and celebrate. We will see how long it lasts," I said with a smirk.

"Just wait, Gigi," Vivian continued. "You will love it. And you will finally be doing something other than waiting around for other folks to make you happy."

"Be quiet, Vivian," I said. "Go check on that turkey—you know you burn it every year."

We laughed again and ended our call.

Over two hours passed and still no Monty. It would have been ridiculous for me to call Stacey back to see if Greg was home, so I waited.

Finally the doorbell rang.

"Hey, Monty!" Isabel greeted with a smile.

"Hey, shortie!"

Monty hugged Isabel as she grabbed the bag of presents from his hand.

"Where is the other one?" he asked while looking at me.

"The other one is right here," Grace answered glibly. "What's up, Montgomery?"

"Nothing much, Grace, and what is *up* with you?"

"All right you two," I interrupted. "Hey there, sweetie."

"Um . . . hey, baby," Monty growled.

Those big strong arms were holding me so tight. It was nice.

"Why didn't you tell me you landed early? I was almost headed to the airport when Stacey called," I asked with a frown, backing away.

"Because he is inconsiderate," Grace concluded.

"Grace!" I yelled, even though she was right.

"It's all right, baby. The knucklehead is right. I was inconsiderate. You know me and Greg have to do our thing. I'm sorry, but I am here now."

I tried to ignore the fact that there were almost three hours from the time I'd spoken to Stacey and the time Monty showed up at our door. I just wanted it to be a peaceful day, a peaceful week. It was good to have my Monty back home.

∽

We spent the week of Monty's visit doing the ordinary stuff that families do. Making dinner together. Playing games with the girls. Football party on Sunday night. Homework, dishes, laundry, errands. Monty and Greg disappeared on their own a few times, which was totally expected of such close friends. On his last night in town, Monty and I met Greg and Stacey for dinner at Greg's favorite Italian restaurant. Since we were already surrounded by the paraphernalia of all things Italian, we couldn't stop talking about our two-week trip to Italy that was just around the corner. The plan was for the two of us to meet in Chicago after I sent the girls to spend the holidays with their father in Indianapolis. Even though Monty would be with family and friends in Indianapolis, I wanted to spend some time with my mom in Chicago, so we decided to meet at O'Hare and fly out together from there.

I must have been trying to get a head start on the trip because I was throwing back glasses of Chianti as if I were sitting at a sidewalk café watching the sun set over the hills of Tuscany. The rest of the night was pretty much a blur. In the true nature of a man's man, Monty managed to get me safely back home and carried me up to the bedroom. Although I was quite smashed from all the wine, I faintly recalled his whispering beautiful words in my ear as he removed my dress and tucked me in for the night. I felt his warm body crawl into bed next to me as his hand worked its way up my inner thigh.

∽

"So what else can you tell me about this new dance class of yours?" Monty asked as we headed to the airport the following morning.

"Monty, you know I love to dance. Stacey and Viv thought it would be something fun for me to try," I replied through the haze of an agonizing hangover.

"How close do you have to be to these men?"

"Oh my goodness—not Mr. Big Balls himself. Are you jealous?" I had to laugh even though I knew my head would pay for it.

"Look, I don't want these dudes getting any ideas just because I'm not in town," Monty said.

"Got it. Well, it takes two, Monty. You trust me, and that is all that matters, right?"

We arrived at the airport and I hopped out of the passenger

seat to drive. Monty gave me his one-of-a-kind bear hug, we kissed, and he was gone again. Not such a tough departure this time. I knew I would see him again in a few weeks.

∾ *Chapter Two*

"I don't have time for this. I don't have time for this," I continued to tell myself as I drove to the community center where stepping classes were held, exactly eight minutes from my house. All I could imagine was that scene from *Love Jones* or that R. Kelly video with a group of super classy folks seriously getting their groove on. How would I possibly fit into any of that? I do love to dance, but keeping the rhythm while you move from side to side was about all I had been doing since I stopped taking ballet classes in college. At least by finally showing up, I would get Vivian and Stacey off my back about it. I was there, so I would go in, spend an hour and a half doing what I was told to do, and then I would leave and resume my everyday life.

As I entered the door of the community center, there was a woman sitting at the reception desk. Before I could ask her where classes were held, a man standing nearby stretched out his hand. "Welcome. Are you here to learn how to step?"

"Um . . . yes?" I answered while shaking his hand. You know the phrase, "tall, dark, and handsome"? Well, let's just say that his picture would be next to the definition in Webster's. He was nicely built, too, pretty athletic.

"You don't sound sure," he said with a wonderful smile. "We will get you going in a few minutes. The line dancing class is about to end."

"Thanks. I'm Gigi, by the way."

"Oh okay, Stacey's girl. Nice to meet you, Gigi. I am Carter Justice. You can call me CJ. I am one of the stepping class instructors."

"Great. Nice to meet you, CJ," I said.

"That will be five dollars."

Strike one . . . Vivian told me the first class was free.

As I entered the classroom, I saw Vivian right away with that big smile of hers. She waved and yelled across the room, "Talk to you after class, Gigi!" I saw her explaining who I was to the woman dancing next to her. There was another group of ladies being led in something called "drills" by a statuesque woman wearing ridiculously high pink heels. It appeared that she was repeatedly instructing them on techniques that they had previously learned, and she was ensuring that everyone was able to grasp the steps and turns at a level she deemed acceptable. "I don't think I would ever want to be in that group," I was again talking to myself. The lady in the pink pumps was definitely a perfectionist. My observations were interrupted by CJ.

"Okay everyone, let's bring it in. Time to step. For those of you who are new to the class, I am Carter Justice, cofounder of Untouchable Steppers. You may have heard about my football career from awhile back, but now I am just CJ, community activist and master stepper."

What the hell is a master stepper? I thought.

"How many beginners today?" CJ asked.

Six of us raised our hands.

"All right, that's beautiful. We will break into groups. My

brother, Cameron, had a gig and couldn't make it tonight, so pardon me while I get the other groups going. I will come back and work with you ladies and you will be dancing in no time."

While CJ turned his attention toward his other students, I continued my classroom investigation. Another group of steppers had begun dancing in a small area near the rear of the classroom. *Wow!* I thought. *This is a really cool dance.* There were four men dancing with four women, and it was obvious that each of them had been dancing for some time. The moves were totally in sync, and the women seemed to know what the men wanted them to do by some sort of telepathy. *What have I gotten myself into?*

"Okay, ladies, let's go to work." CJ had made his way back over to my group of beginners.

"Since this group is new to the dance, I always like to take a few minutes to give you a better understanding of the vibrant and diverse history of stepping."

CJ explained that the dance that had become known as "Chicago Stepping" originated in the city of Chicago and had derived from several African American dance forms, including the Lindy Hop, the jitterbug, the swing, and the bop, to name a few. The dance involved two or more people dancing as partners to the sounds of any music with a steppers' beat: jazz, soul, funk, R&B, neo soul, reggae, or rap music. Steppers' dances and parties are called "sets," and attire can range from ragtime to black tie, or any other unique style of contemporary fashion better known as "Steppers Sharp."

"All right, now that the history lesson is over, the dance that you will begin to learn today is called Chicago Style Eight Count Steppin'. There are several variations of the dance—original, old school, new school, and freestyle. Some with a six count, some with no count. The eight count is considered a 'new school' version of the dance and is called the 'eight count' because each step, turn, and combination that you will execute is taken in synchronization with your partner to an eight-count beat. In other words, you will be *stepping* to a count of *eight*. The first thing you ladies have to understand is the beat of the dance. It is not a fast count of eight, and it is not a slow and steady count of eight. Listen to the drum . . . one, two, three . . . four, five, six . . . seven, eight. One, two, three . . . four, five, six . . . seven, eight. You might have to listen to music a little differently than you have before. Once you become accustomed to feeling the music, the rest will follow. Okay, let's move our feet to the same count. Starting on the left and alternating with the right: one, two, three . . . four, five, six . . . seven, eight. One . . . Four . . . Seven . . ."

Oh my goodness . . . is this for real? How do I turn this simple march into these smooth, seamless steps I see happening all around me? Only an hour to go.

"Good," CJ continued. "Keep it going, ladies."

After about ten minutes of rhythmic marching, I watched CJ motion to one of the women in the group being led by the lady in the pink shoes. He pulled two of the women from my group of six beginners and said, "Work with these two on the beat of the drum."

And then there were four. I wasn't quite sure where I was supposed to be after only ten minutes, but I suppose I had arrived.

"Now that you have somewhat of a grasp on the count and the beat of the dance, we are going to put a little sway to your step. This move is called *the basic*. It is the fundamental eight-count move that serves as the foundation for the entire dance. Standing with your feet a little less than shoulder width apart, start with your left foot . . ."

As I tried to pay attention to the instruction CJ was giving, I couldn't help but take another look around the room. I was in awe of the graceful movements between the dancers. Well, most of them anyway. I noticed there was one guy in particular who was all over the place. At any rate, I started to become a little bit angry with myself that I hadn't started stepping a year ago when Stacey first invited me. *I would be spinning, flowing, and dancing with that group,* I thought. Instead I was stuck marching up and down, feeling like a robot trying to move its feet in unnatural directions.

When I snapped out of my daydream and realized I hadn't been listening to CJ's directions, I thought for sure I was about to be called over to join in the fate of the two who had left my group a few minutes ago. They were still marching in place. Then CJ continued.

"Again, one . . . two . . . put the three back . . . four . . . five . . . six back home, seven-eight. Again . . ."

For the next fifteen minutes or so, our tiny group practiced that basic step to about five songs. By the fourth song, the steps felt a little less robotic to me and were starting to smooth out. *Hmm . . . not too bad,* I thought, *I'll be in that group over there in no time at all.* And then CJ grabbed my hands.

"Now, I want you to begin to feel the man's signals."

Oh shit.

"You have to understand that another fundamental principle of the art of stepping is that the man leads the dance. In other words, he will give you what we call *signals.* Your partner will give you directions using both tension in his hand movements and his body placement in order to tell you what he wants you to do or where he wants you to go. It's Gigi, right?"

"Yes," I whispered.

"Give me your basic. One, two, three . . . four, five, six . . . seven, eight. Good, now by my gently pulling your arms in this swaying motion, you know that I want you to do your basic as you have just learned it. What if I stand in front of you and pull you toward me?"

"I walk toward you?"

"Right, but keep your count. One, two, three . . . four, five, six . . . seven, eight. Now walk back. One, two, three . . . four, five, six . . . seven, eight. Good!"

Oh my goodness, it was over. Thank God I didn't make a complete fool of myself. As CJ moved down the line working individually with the beginners, I noticed that there were only ten minutes of class remaining. It wasn't nearly as bad as I had imagined it would be. Not bad at all.

"Let's bring it in," CJ announced. "Thank you to everyone who came out to class tonight. It is always wonderful to see both new and returning faces. Everyone put your hands together for our new folks. We hope to see you all again next week. If you continue to come, you will learn that this dance fosters a community of unity in a mature, fun, and positive atmosphere."

As I walked out of class, Vivian caught up to me.

"So what did you think?" She could hardly wait to know.

"It was . . . interesting," I told her.

"Will you come back? I saw you smiling over there when CJ grabbed your hands."

"Why weren't you paying closer attention to what you were supposed to be doing?" I heckled. "What's CJ's story anyway? He mentioned something about football?"

"I will have to fill you in later. I need to get home. My kids have been trying to track me down for the last half hour. Call Stacey and we can all meet for a drink and talk about class. She knows CJ better than I do anyway! Tell the girls I said 'hi.'"

Whenever Vivian told me she had to "fill me in later," I knew there was a story to follow. I must admit that I was more than a bit intrigued by this new world of dancing. I had already decided that I was definitely going back to class.

∽

"Don't keep me in suspense. What did you think of your first class?" Stacey asked when she called me a few hours later.

"It was okay," I answered. "It wasn't as bad as I expected. I will go one step further and say it was kinda fun."

"Well you know once you start, stepping is pretty addictive.

Something about being on that dance floor, spinning and flowing . . . " Stacey started before I interrupted her.

"I was marching. There was no flow involved of any kind," I said.

"You'll get there. Just give it a few months."

My phone beeped with another call.

"Let me call you back later, sweetie," I said to Stacey. "Monty's on the other line."

"How was your dance class, baby?" Monty asked.

"It was fun," I replied. "Different than any other type of dance I have learned. I think you would like it since you love being in charge. In stepping, the man *leads* the dance."

"I just bet they do," Monty sneered.

"We had this conversation, Monty. There is absolutely nothing for you to be grumbling about." I changed the subject. "I am getting so excited about Italy! Only a few weeks to go."

"I know, baby, it will be a trip we will never forget," Monty said. Then he hesitated a few seconds before asking, "Do you think you are going back to stepping class?"

"I have only been to one class, sweetie. I would never hear the end of it from Stacey and Viv if I quit already. Besides, it gets me out of the house and gives me something to do *for me*, aside from working, running behind the girls, and waiting for you to come visit—all things I love to do, by the way. But who knows, the next time you see me, I may have given it up altogether."

Why was I lying to him like that?

"Hmm . . . time will tell," Monty said.

∽ *Chapter Three*

The week had flown by, and it was already time for my second stepping class. I wondered if it was normal that I had been practicing my basic step in front of the mirror at least twice a day over the last week. This time both Stacey and Vivian would be there, so it would be good to see smiling, familiar faces. As I walked into the community center, I noticed a few of my fellow newbies in the hallway waiting to go into class. I met Sasha, a forty-five-year-old fifth-grade schoolteacher who, not unlike me, decided it was time to add some fun to her life. She had been married for seven years but had no children. She met CJ at a community event about two years ago and had attended a few steppers sets to check out the scene.

I also met Eleana. She was thirty-nine and single, and she actually admitted out loud that she started stepping to find a man.

"I have been on the singles scene for the last five years, and the eligible assortment of the opposite sex is scarce at best," Eleana said. "These days a man either wants you to take care of him or he wants you to let him run your life. There doesn't seem to be anything in between. Don't get me wrong, the dance is cool, but I had to explore some other options for—"

Eleana was interrupted by the sound of a man clearing his throat.

"Ahem," he started, "excuse me, ladies," he said as he reached for the door of the classroom. He had a bit of a smirk on his face, as if he had overheard the juicy parts of our conversation. Our eyes met only for a second, but it was long enough for me to notice that he had a nice smile. Just then, the doors opened and the lady in the pink shoes invited us in.

"Sorry line dancing ran a little late, ladies, but you are always welcome to join in," she said. "C'mon in, Harp." The lady in pink held the door open for the man in the hall.

"CJ and Cameron are not here yet, so I will get class started," she said as we entered the room.

We gathered in a circle.

"For those of you I haven't met, my name is Ivy Prince. I lead the line dance class held an hour before this stepping class begins. You beginners may be asking yourselves: Why is there a line dance class right before stepping, and why is a Black woman teaching it? We are not talking about country line dancing; we are talking about *soul* line dancing here. Think about the Bus Stop or the Electric Slide that our parents used to do back in the seventies. Soul line dancing uses repeated sequences of steps to create a choreographed group dance to R&B music—or sometimes I throw in a little pop or even disco."

Following her introduction, Ivy split the groups as CJ had done a week earlier. Sasha, Eleana, and I were the only returning newcomers from the last class. Across the room, I saw Stacey already dancing with John, one of CJ's assistants.

"Hey, Gigi!" I caught Stacey's eye midturn.

Vivian then turned around and waved with a smile.

"Last week you ladies began learning your basic step. Let's see how much you remember," Ivy directed.

Ivy stood with her back to us and began counting out the basic step. We followed her foot patterns for two songs. I think all three of us must have found ourselves counting to eight whenever we heard music playing during the past week.

"You ladies are ready to learn your first turn!" Ivy concluded. "It is called a *right turn*. No surprise by the name, you make a full turn to your right. It is not a turn in place, however. You will take two steps forward toward your partner and begin turning to the right on three. Let me show you."

Ivy demonstrated the turn twice.

"That looks about right to me." I heard a familiar male voice.

"Cam!" Ivy exclaimed. "Come over here and help these new ladies learn their right turns."

Cam . . . as in Cameron? Wait a minute . . . no one told me CJ and his brother were twins!

"Hello, ladies. My name is Cameron Justice. I bet I don't have to tell you that I am CJ's brother."

The resemblance was remarkable. Same voice, same muscular, athletic build, even the same walk. Unlike CJ, Cameron wore a very well-kept mustache and goatee.

"Let's see what my brother has taught you ladies," he said with a smile.

He went down our short row of three in very much the same pattern that CJ had shown us a week earlier. Not only was he checking to see if we remembered our basic step, but he was also sure to introduce himself personally to each of us before he took our hands.

"Okay, nice. Let's work on that right turn that Ivy was beginning to show you when I came in."

At that moment, CJ showed up and headed toward a group of more advanced dancers on the other side of the room. When he saw Cam working with our group, CJ motioned Cam to join him near the front of the class.

"Excuse me, ladies," Cam said. "My big brother, only by about two minutes, beckons."

Cam left our group to meet CJ.

I couldn't hear what they were saying, but the body language told me it wasn't exactly a friendly conversation.

"I got this," Cam said as he made his way back to our group.

"Now where were we, ladies?" Cam said. "Ah yes, our right turn. As Ivy explained, two steps toward me, and then my signal will guide you into the rest of the turn. Gigi, let's demonstrate."

Cameron took me by both hands and gently pulled me forward. Suddenly I was turning to my right on my third step and clumsily landed back in front of him to finish my count of eight.

He smiled and I smiled back. I was actually having a good time.

"Not bad for a first try." Cam tried to sound sincere.

"Let's put some work into that turn to make sure that you are ready to move on. The count of eight is important in understanding how the dance works with a partner, but balance and feeling the music become even more critical as your skills improve."

I looked up more than once only to notice that CJ was glaring in our direction from time to time. What was that about?

By the end of class, the three of us had the right turn down to a science. I felt like a ballerina all over again but way cooler. But it was more than that. Even though it was only my second class, I began to realize that for the entire length of that four-minute song, I, Gigi Grant, had been the center of someone's attention. I hadn't truly been the center of attention for as long as I could remember. And it felt absolutely wonderful.

"Let's bring it in," CJ requested. "Nice to see some of my newcomers have returned for a second class. Did my brother take care of you ladies?"

"He most certainly did!" Eleana replied, smiling from ear to ear, batting her heavily shadowed eyes at Cam.

Damn, girl, show a little restraint, I thought. I was no longer the slightest bit surprised by our conversation in the hallway before class.

"Good to hear," CJ said. I hoped to flash a smile of my own after enjoying my practice turn with Cam, but I couldn't find him anywhere. He must have disappeared from the room soon after CJ asked if he "took care" of us.

Aside from the facial hair and choice of attire, Cam and

CJ were identical, physically speaking. But after only five minutes of Cam holding my hands, I began to notice a difference between them. Just couldn't quite put my finger on it.

ᵒᵉᵒ

"*Twins*, Stacey! Really? You didn't think I needed to know that part?" I scolded my friend.

"Relax, G. I thought you knew!" Stacey replied casually as she sipped her Merlot.

Stacey and I sat at our favorite bar in the cities—halfway between her home and mine. A casual, dark, and quiet hole-in-the-wall where we could truly relax. And much like the patrons of *Cheers*, the waitstaff knew us by name.

"I have been showing you pictures of steppers for years now," Stacey continued. "I can't believe you never noticed."

"I most certainly did not," I assured her in my artificially astonished tone of voice.

Stacey giggled. "Well, you get two for the price of one, and they are certainly not tough to look at. Besides all that, they really are good people and they both love that dance . . . in their own way and for their own reasons."

"Well, what else have you neglected to tell me? CJ mentioned something about football and once said that Cam was missing class because he had a gig."

"What time is Viv getting here?"

"Vivian had to pick her son up from football practice. She will be here in about ten minutes. Wait a minute—why are you trying to distract me?"

Stacey laughed harder this time as she ordered her second glass of wine and began to tell me all she had learned about the brothers during the last four years.

Carter and Cameron Justice were born and raised in Chicago, Illinois. They moved to Minneapolis about ten years ago after their parents passed on. They were the only children of a father who was an aspiring jazz musician and a mother who was a schoolteacher. Carter was divorced and had an adult son who lived in Chicago. Cameron had never been married and had no children. Although both brothers were heavily involved in athletics in their youth, Carter, who quickly became known as "CJ," was the one who excelled in football. He was an outstanding tight end in high school and was recruited to play for at least five universities that were renowned for their football teams. When it was time to choose a school, CJ decided to stay closer to home and accepted a football scholarship to Notre Dame so that he could help care for his ailing mother. After college, he was drafted by the Chicago Bears and played for four years until a severe knee injury abruptly ended his career.

Although he possessed the same amount of athletic prowess, Cameron, on the other hand, decided to follow in his father's footsteps by becoming a musician. He tried his hand at several instruments, but at the end of the day, he discovered that the trumpet was his passion. The twins' father was a saxophonist who played now and again in several small venues around Chicago, but he was never actually able to make a living at it. Cameron, on the other hand, had been successful at making a career out of his music. He wrote and produced for local jazz artists and was often booked for performances in both the Twin Cities and Chicago. In fact, Cam was the impetus for the brothers' relocation because of the wealth of potential opportunities in the Minneapolis music scene.

Sports and music aside, both Cam and CJ were also naturally born businessmen. Both received their college degrees in business, although Cam's education ultimately focused more on the music industry. It was to no one's surprise that they would someday start a business that had an impact on both the arts and the community.

Stacey continued with a story about how CJ once told her that the brothers were raised to live a modest life. They were taught that no matter how little they seemed to have at times, they should always make it a priority to give back to the community in which they lived. I again recalled that Stacey met CJ when they served together on the board of one of her nonprofits. She appeared to be totally convinced that their family upbringing was the reason CJ had been so involved in the community and supportive of various worthy causes.

The brothers became active in the stepping community years before they left their hometown. They had introduced the dance to hundreds of people in the Twin Cities since moving here and creating their organization, Untouchable Steppers of Minnesota. Stacey told me that when the brothers made their trips back home, they attended workshops and continued to share skills and techniques with other steppers who were well known for their talent in the birthplace of Chicago Stepping.

"Both CJ and Cam are great at commissioning the stepping community to hold demonstrations and fund-raisers to increase awareness of important issues in our communities. CJ, in particular, has been a great resource for me," Stacey continued. "Whenever I need to bounce ideas off him for some of my board work, he always has a phenomenally creative point of view. Then we barter and trade and I help him with publicity for his next event."

"That's cool," I acknowledged. "But let me ask you . . . did I notice a little friction between the two of them during class?"

"You know how family can be, Gigi. Especially *brothers*. Men are always going to be men."

So that was it? They were two nice, college-educated boys born and raised to have honest careers and give back to their community? I supposed that was possible, but I had a hunch that there was much more to learn and that it wouldn't take too long for me to find out for myself.

ᴄᴏ Chapter Four

New client meeting downtown. Running late. I had spent another all-nighter on the phone with Monty, so I was already short on sleep. On top of that, Isabel couldn't decide whether her purple jeans or her turquoise jeans looked better with her blue and gray shirt. That automatically translated to Isabel spending an extra thirty minutes in front of the mirror, and Gigi being thirty minutes late to a meeting.

Parking downtown was always a nightmare. At least there was no snow on the ground, even though it was early December. As I was searching for a spot on the street amid inattentive holiday shoppers, I was suddenly taken back to six years ago when I worked for the largest interior design firm in town. Ah, the perks. Prepaid parking. Three-hour lunches. Trips to New York, LA, and even Italy to conduct "research" on the latest trends in interior design and explore the origins of architectural creativity. All while dining at five-star restaurants and enjoying lavish hotel accommodations on Park Avenue and Rodeo Drive. Sometimes it made me wonder why I left to do my own thing. Oh yeah . . . my baby girls needed their mom. And let's not forget the politics, the egos, and the assholes. Now I was beginning to remember clearly. Once I decided that I wasn't going to sleep with the head of the firm to land the next trip to Paris, things kinda went downhill from there.

Found a spot two blocks away with eight whole minutes to spare.

"Hey!" someone was yelling as my high heels hurried their way through the middle of the street with portfolio under one arm, handbag on the other, iPhone in hand, banana in my mouth. A rumbling stomach makes a bad first impression, trust me.

Ordinarily I don't turn around or respond in any fashion to a random "hey" on the street. But I heard it a second time.

"Hey, *stepper!*"

Okay. I had been to that stepping class twice and I was already being branded a stepper? I stopped and turned around.

"How's it going? You look like you're in a hurry."

No shit, Sherlock. I recognized him from class. He was the guy with the smirk who had interrupted Eleana's rendition of *a tale of too few eligible men* before class last week.

"You're observant. I am less than seven minutes away from being late to meet a new client," I explained, trying my best not to spit banana in his face.

"Mind if I walk with you? Let me carry a bag for you. I don't have to be at work for another twenty minutes," he spoke softly and motioned for my portfolio.

"Thank you. I have seen you in class, but we haven't met. I'm Gigi. Is it . . . Harp?"

"Harper. Harper Drake. CJ calls me Harp. Obviously, I have seen you in class once or twice myself. CJ usually asks me to dance with the more experienced steppers, so I don't always get the opportunity to meet the new dancers for a few months. He can be pretty territorial over newcomers."

He pretended to make a joke of it, but I could tell he meant what he was saying.

"Well, nice to officially meet you, Harper." I smiled as I was beginning to notice what a cutie he was. His appearance was very neat. Nicely pressed slacks and a sweater, polished shoes, and an ivy cap, like a newsboy but much more stylish. And that smile. Definitely remembered that smile from class last week.

"Nice to meet you too, Gigi. Do you have a last name?"

"Grant," I muttered as I finally finished my banana, now trying to collect myself and straighten my skirt which had shifted off-center from my hurried walk.

"Okay then. I will see you in class, Ms. Grant. Enjoy the rest of your day and hope you have a productive meeting."

Harper returned my portfolio, smiled, and turned to walk in the direction from which we came. All the while I was thinking *seems like a nice guy*, the only thing that kept resonating in my mind were Vivian's words: "Whatever you do, Gigi, don't get involved with any of those steppers." Needed to have a chat with Viv and gather a little intel on Mr. Harper Drake.

⁓

"You ran into Harper downtown?" Vivian almost shrieked as she placed her cake in the oven.

"That's what I said. What's the big deal? He seemed perfectly nice," I surmised.

"Maybe you should wait and talk to Stace, but I have heard some things about Harp," Viv replied, leaning over her kitchen counter with her hands on her ears.

"I bet you have, Viv. Let me guess. He is a womanizer and has had every woman in stepping class. He has no job, no car, and lives with his mother, sister, or auntie. And he is looking for a woman to take care of him."

"Shut the front door, G," Viv exclaimed in phony astonishment. "How did you know?"

Vivian was clearly trying to pretend that she hadn't told me that same exact story about every man that I had ever asked her about.

"Girl, something is really wrong with you." I giggled. "Seriously, do you know anything about him?"

"Not really, Gigi," Vivian finally admitted. "I bet Stacey knows him a little better since she has been dancing longer. He is pretty quiet, but he always seems nice. I think he dated a few women in the circle, but I can't even be sure of that, just rumors. And you know how women like to go on and on about things that may or may not have ever happened. Personally, like I already told you, I don't trust any of those men who step. I have heard too many stories and seen too many women get disrespected, not only by men, but by each other! And we both know that I am far too cute to be fighting somebody, especially over some dude."

"Geez, Vivian," I started, "if there is so much craziness involved in this dance, why do you keep stepping?"

"Probably for the same reason as you, Gigi," Vivian answered as sincerely as I had ever heard her. "Because you can escape from everything else while you are dancing."

Vivian was right.

"Now quit trying to change the subject! Harper certainly must have caught your eye for you to be asking about him." Vivian grinned, showing all of her teeth.

"He seemed like a nice guy . . . and he is a cute one." I admitted. "I am just curious. Besides, I have a boyfriend."

"Uh-huh. Sure, G. Oh wait!" Vivian stopped. "I know that Harper is going to be in the twins' stepping contest in a few months with that Latina chica. Eva is her *nombre*," Vivian said in the worst Spanish accent I had ever heard. "She started stepping five or six months before you."

"Okay, so what? Does that mean something?"

"No, not really. Some dancing partners are usually a couple *off* the dance floor, that's all. It doesn't mean anything. But like you said, you have a *boyfriend*, remember?"

That was Vivian, always trying to start some stuff when there was no stuff to start. I could hardly wait to call Stacey.

Stacey told me that Harper Drake was the ideal personification of the stepping world. Always neat and well groomed, carrying himself as if he were the perfect gentleman. Medium build and handsome, not drop dead gorgeous, but definitely handsome. Probably a guy who loved to be surrounded by women, but really didn't have much experience with them. Forty-something years old and considered himself a resource for new steppers. He hooked up with the brothers as a fill-in helper/instructor about three years ago. He came and went to classes and workshops as he pleased, but he was fully committed to the dance when he was around. Stacey

unable to attend and report their findings to the brothers. Don't get me wrong, I can't be sure if it was by order of either CJ or Cam. I honestly believed that this group of women was absolutely certain that espionage was their solemn duty and self-inflicted method of expressing allegiance to the twins. It pains me to admit this, as I do my very best to respect all women, but trust me when I say that there was no more accurate description for this collection of the female species, no ifs, ands, or buts about it. Can't even point to a particular race, religion, class, or creed. These seven covered the spectrum of both the rainbow and the economy.

The Furious Five, on the other hand, were all from the same side of town, they all shopped in the same places, they hardly ever came to class, and, when they did, they all had perfectly horrific attitude problems. DeAnn led this illustrious group, none of whom believed in the saying taught to us by our mothers: if you don't have anything nice to say, don't say anything at all. Those five had something negative to say about everything and everyone at every event. But believe it or not, they appeared to be totally harmless, just absolutely furious all the time. Lips twisted, eyes rolling, and they never held their tongues. It was no wonder that one of the Five's biggest complaints was that they were rarely asked to dance at steppers sets. Can you imagine such a thing? If there was a positive side to this uncompromising group, you never had to question where you stood with them. If one of them liked you, they all liked you and you knew it . . . somehow. But if they didn't, well, you knew that, too.

Now understand that this is just to name a few of the

most entertaining members of the cast. There were more than four dozen women, and about ten men, who appeared to be current faithful followers of the twins. I was told that the number of followers was a sizeable decrease from the hundred who at one time regularly supported the brothers, but still the degree of devotion was practically unfathomable. I thought about how the knights of ancient times must have felt when pledging their loyalty to the kings of old. Even absent the seemingly irrational level of dedication, the almost ten-to-one ratio of women to men alone was enough to send someone like me running and screaming in the opposite direction. But I didn't run. *I can avoid the drama,* I told myself. And for the first time in a long time, I was having fun.

∞ *Chapter Five*

It was the end of the last stepping class before the Christmas holiday. As we stood listening to announcements at the end of the session, CJ reminded us of the New Year's Eve set and encouraged all of his new steppers to attend.

"It will be a chance for you to showcase your new skills in a safe and fun environment with no pressure. We will all be there to dance with you—me, Cam, John, Harp, and Michael."

I quickly tuned out of the conversation because all I could think about was how quickly I could finish packing for my trip to Italy. Monty and I were scheduled to leave in less than a week and I could hardly wait.

∞

Christmas week had come and gone, and the girls and I had finally made it to the airport. As was generally the case when my daughters and I traveled, we were always late getting to the airport, we were always overpacked, and we always managed to charm the security personnel into allowing us ahead of other passengers to make our flight in time.

The plan was to head to Chicago. The girls' dad would meet us at the airport and drive them to his home in Indianapolis. My sister was coming to pick me up from O'Hare to hang out in Chicago with her and our mom before I met Monty back at the airport the following day. When we arrived at our gate inside the Minneapolis–St. Paul International Airport, we were told that our flight had been cancelled for bad weather which was headed for Chicago.

Talk about disappointment. After speaking with four separate airline agents, I learned that there was a flight that had been routed around the storm and actually landed in Indianapolis instead of Chicago. It was scheduled to leave in about two hours. Even though it would take another hour in the air because we would have to now fly through Atlanta, at least our plans would only be altered by a few hours instead of an entire day. I never liked to make things easier for my ex-husband, but if I was able to reach out to everyone and let them know about the change, I would just consider it my Christmas present to him. And on top of everything else, I would get to connect with Monty a day early. Bonus for Gigi.

∽

The hours in the air were pretty uneventful. The girls were engaged in their usual flight activities. Grace was deep into the music on her iPad while simultaneously watching a movie, as Isabel dozed in and out of consciousness with her headphones on her ears, occasionally waking to take a picture of the clouds.

I, on the other hand, was brushing up on my Italian. By "brushing up" I mean trying to learn it. How hard could it be?

I had had six years of Spanish in high school and college. Simply change the letter *a* to an *o* now and again and I figured it was pretty intuitive. I had been to Italy years ago on business, but this trip was all about the romance. We were scheduled to join a tour led by a local guide so that Monty and I wouldn't be entirely unsupervised and would hopefully avoid getting into too much international trouble. Rome, Venice, Tuscany. This trip was definitely going to take our relationship to a new level.

Landed safely in Indianapolis. My daughters' father met us at baggage claim.

"Enjoy your trip," he said.

"Thanks, I will," I replied. "Love you guys! Give me hugs and kisses and I will see you in two weeks."

"Bye, Mom. I'll miss you," Isabel said, giving me a huge hug.

"Have a good time and bring me back some gelato," Grace replied, hugging me tightly.

Then she whispered in my ear, "Too bad you're spending two whole weeks with that ratchet, Monty."

"Love you, too, Gracie," I replied with a smirk.

And then they were off.

It was about six o'clock in the evening and I was pretty exhausted from the day of travel. I had met Monty's Indianapolis cousin, Christopher, last time I was there, so I decided to take a cab to his home, where Monty told me he would be staying. Even though I had sent him several text messages and called a few times, I hadn't been able to connect with Monty to let him know about the change of plans. I was sure I could catch him in Indianapolis before he headed to Chicago the next day to meet me for our flight to Italy.

As the cab pulled up in front of the house, Christopher was just arriving home. The look of surprise on his face was priceless.

"Gigi! What are you doing here?" Christopher asked.

"Nice to see you, too, Christopher," I answered.

"Oh my bad, babe," Christopher said with a smile as he leaned into the cab window to kiss me on the cheek. "I just meant we weren't expecting you."

"Well, the weather changed our plans, so I ended up flying the girls all the way here," I explained. "I've been trying to reach Monty to let him know I was headed here, but I haven't heard back from him."

"Oh," Christopher replied.

He grabbed my bags from the trunk; I finished paying the cab driver and started to head toward the front door.

"I'm not sure Monty is here, Gigi," Christopher said.

"His truck is right there," I said, pointing to Monty's white pickup.

"Yeah, I know, but he may not be home right now," Christopher reiterated.

"Then I will wait for him inside, Chris," I said, hurrying to get out of the cold.

As I walked inside Christopher's house, I removed my boots and took a seat at the kitchen counter. Christopher offered me a glass of wine to warm up. Just as I was about to accept that offer of a drink, I heard voices.

"Who's upstairs?" I asked.

"Not sure," Christopher replied.

"What do you mean you're not sure? This is *your* house, Chris!" I replied.

The next sound I heard was Monty's laugh. I glared at Christopher, hopped off of that kitchen barstool, and immediately made my way up the stairs.

"Gigi!" I heard Christopher from the bottom of the stairs, but he knew it was pointless.

I flung open the door of the room where I heard voices to find Monty. It would have been a pretty nice photo actually. Mouths wide open make perfect targets for a dart board. He was in bed, not with one, but with two women. I shut the door, careful not to slam it, descended the staircase, and proceeded to finish my first glass of wine with a single swig. Christopher poured me a second glass in silence while I waited for my cab to the airport.

Chapter Six

Minneapolis seemed frostier than normal as I walked to my car following a particularly unsuccessful client meeting. The evening air was icy and crisp while the downtown skyline was carefully concealed behind weighty gray clouds ready to produce a fresh snowfall. Suddenly I was no longer thinking about the fact that I didn't land the account with a new client. It was New Year's Eve.

The holidays were behind me and a new year was about to begin. I was still wallowing in self-pity over the end of a relationship full of lies, deceit, degradation, humiliation, stress . . . and great sex. Pretty unhealthy stuff, but I still had every right to be angry. In fact, I didn't know if I was more angry about the breakup with Monty or missing the trip to Italy. Stacey told me that Greg told her that Monty rebooked the trip from Italy to some island off the coast of the Caribbean, found a cheaper rate, and took both of those tramps slumming in his bed in Indiana. How had I gotten mixed up with a guy who would do that? Nevermind. I knew that answer. I had clearly assumed the risk in that relationship. So maybe the better question was: Did he think I was the kind of woman who would be okay with that? Hmm. Note to self: continue to work on carrying yourself in a manner that does not attract Neanderthals. In any case, I didn't want to see or deal with anything or anyone until my fists had time to unclench themselves. Nonetheless, Ms. Vivian Monroe absolutely insisted that I attend the twins' New Year's Eve set tonight. I had been to class exactly five times, and on top of being an emotional wreck, she wanted me to dance in public.

"Gigi," Vivian tried to reason with me, "you already knew that Monty was a damn cheater. I know that may not make it any easier, but Stacey told you—"

"I know, I know," I stopped her midsentence.

"Well, act like a grown-ass woman and get yourself together! How long are you gonna sit around pouting? It is the beginning of a new year, and I am not going to let you sit home alone like you're all torn up over someone who isn't worth your energy."

"Hold on a minute, Viv. Stacey is calling my other line."

I clicked over.

"Hey, girl." I could hear Stacey's smile.

"Hold on, Stacey. Viv's on the other line. Before I add her back in, will you talk some sense into her and tell her I'm not ready to go out? Especially on New Year's Eve," I pleaded with my friend.

"Just add her in, sweetie," Stacey requested.

I tapped the conference icon on my phone. "Stacey, Viv?"

"Hell yes I am here," Vivian chimed in first. "Hey, Stace, can you believe Gigi is trying not to come out tonight? Giving me some story about how she is *sad* and upset."

"Well, Viv, Gigi is entitled to her feelings," Stacey tried to reason.

"What the hell? You are letting him win, Gigi." I could hear the fury in Vivian's tone. "You know what? In all the years I have known you, I have always admired how strong you are and how you have never let any man in your life walk all over you and the girls. Monty was doing both of those things."

"Look, you two," I finally spoke. "Understand that this isn't one hundred percent about Monty. Yep, he screwed me over, but I am just exhausted with the game entirely. I have been single for ten years *by choice.* You both know firsthand that I could have been married three or four times over by now if I wanted to."

"There is absolutely no need to brag about it," Vivian said in a mock harsh tone.

"Seriously," I continued. "Of course I knew Monty was a jerk, but he swept me off my feet so high and so fast like no guy had in a very long time. I think that is what made the fall so hard. I can't even say that I am hurting. I think I am still in shock. So believe me when I say I am okay. It's just that this bottle of wine and box of chocolates sound better tonight than a fancy dress and a bunch of people I hardly know."

"I hear you, sis," Stacey added. "But listen, it is exactly six hours before the start of a new year. You know that we are not going to let you sit at home alone."

"And I for one will not be sitting at home with you," Vivian said with certainty.

"Thanks for the support, Vivian." I hoped she could see me rolling my eyes through the phone.

"You know CJ is expecting his new steppers to come to the set. And I hear you've really been picking up the basic dance. *And* I saw Harper trying to show you that dip in class last week," Stacey announced in a schoolgirl tone with a little bit of a giggle.

"Oh yes," Vivian added. "I too saw *the dip*."

I smiled inside and out while Vivian and Stacey continued to tease me.

"Well, I do have a dress."

"Thank *God*. Finally coming to your senses!" Vivian sounded relieved. "I'll swing by and pick you up around ten."

"Excellent, ladies," Stacey affirmed. "You know Greg is traveling, so I will meet you both there. I told CJ that I would help him work the door, so I need to be there in a few hours."

How do they do that? But I knew they were right. It was time I stopped brooding and left the past behind. What better way to ring in my new year than with two of my absolutely favorite people?

∞

Vivian and I arrived to the set around ten fifteen. As I walked into the ballroom, I felt like I had taken a trip about twenty-five years back in time to my senior prom. The room was filled with streamers and balloons, and it seemed like every table sparkled. I made a beeline to the bar and ordered a glass of wine.

"Nice to see you made it, Gigi!" Ivy said with a big smile. She was wearing a long black dress and, of course, extremely high pink heels.

"Have a wonderful time and make sure you get out there on that dance floor!"

"I don't think I will have a choice," I joked.

Stacey was still working the front door, but Vivian had taken a seat at a table with Sasha and three other women. The Secret Seven were strategically scattered about the room so that they could catch any suspicious rumblings and report back to the brothers. The Furious Five, on the other hand, were all seated together at a table as close to the dance floor as humanly possible. No doubt that table was selected so they could have the prime location to deliver accurate critiques of everyone's dance, outfit, and anything else worth criticizing.

I took a seat at the table and looked around to take it all in. There were about one hundred people in the room, and I recognized about fifteen of them. I had just taken a sip from my glass when CJ tapped me on the shoulder.

"You ready?" he asked with a smile.

"Absolutely not," I responded in as serious a tone as I could muster.

"Ha! C'mon. You are *my* new student, so I have to show people what you have been learning," CJ reasoned.

I took a few more quick sips of my wine and stood from the table.

"Go get him, Gigi!" Vivian cheered.

When we arrived at the dance floor, I tried to take myself back to class, imagining that no one else was in the room. Tough to do when disco lights, balloons, and brightly colored zoot suits were creating quite the distraction. I felt my feet moving to the count of eight and CJ guiding me through the basic moves and the four turns I had learned in the exactly seven and a half hours of class time I had under my belt. Before I knew it, the song was over and I had not crashed and burned. CJ gave me a hug with a congratulatory "nice job" and began to escort me back to my seat.

About halfway there, John, the twins' "first knight," motioned for me to join him on the dance floor. I felt a bit more confident now, so I turned and headed back to the floor, which had become much more crowded. As I mentioned earlier, I always felt safe dancing with John. He led me pretty smoothly through the same moves I had performed with CJ. Toward the end of our dance, he tried to signal me into a left spin, which was the move I was just beginning to learn during the last class I attended. I wobbled a bit, but he kept me steady, and then the dance was over.

"Whew, close one!" I said with a sigh of relief.

John nodded with a slight grin and walked me back to my seat.

I was on my second glass of wine, chatting it up with the girls, when I saw Cam on the dance floor. His moves were so much more graceful than CJ's. He seemed to glide across the floor as if he were on roller skates. Don't get me wrong, CJ was a great dancer, but it was almost as if Cam became one with the music.

A few more songs played and Vivian told me that DeAnn, the leader of the Furious Five, asked her about me. "Who is this new girl? What is her name? How long has she been stepping?" were a few of the questions she had asked.

"I told her mean, turned-up-nosed self that she could introduce herself to you and ask her own questions," Viv said.

"I think that was the right thing to tell her," I agreed. "Besides, that is the best way for them to make an informed group decision as to whether or not they can tolerate me!"

Viv and I were smack in the middle of a rather boisterous laugh when Cam took my hand. As he led me to the dance floor, I began to get nervous again. Cam was so smooth on the dance floor that I was sure I was going to look completely mechanical.

Surprisingly, Cam did not let me get too far away from him. He led me through some basic moves, but the song was so slow that it almost felt like an old-fashioned slow drag with a few turns thrown into the mix. It was totally easy. He flashed that gorgeous grin and told me to relax.

After my dance with Cameron, I noticed Harper standing at the door. He had just arrived to the set. It was about twenty minutes until midnight. He was all decked out in a checkered blazer, slacks, and a purple bow tie.

"May I have this dance?" Harper bowed slightly and extended his hand.

"Absolutely, kind sir." I answered, just as goofy as could be. "But I must warn you that I am a danger on the dance floor."

"I'm not worried about it," Harper reassured.

When we made our way to the dance floor, I felt as though every eye was on us. I was once again totally nervous and reminded Harper that I had only been to five classes. As soon as he put his arm around my waist and took my hand in his, I was okay. The song was slow in tempo, so I was thrilled that I didn't have to move quickly to keep up with the beat of the music. I had only danced with Harper twice before in class, most recently when the infamous dip occurred that Stacey and Vivian were teasing me about earlier.

"You're doing really well. Just keep your hands where I can get to them," Harper gently instructed.

As the song ended, he accompanied me back to my table. Stacey had finally stopped working and made it inside. Both she and Vivian had gotten up to line dance, so Harper sat with me while we watched. Since we were alone, I was certain that I had consumed enough liquid courage to ask a few questions of my own about Mr. Drake.

"It's almost midnight, Harper. Where is your date?" I asked.

"I could ask you the same thing, couldn't I?"

"I suppose you could, but I asked you first."

Real mature, Gigi.

"My girlfriend and I couldn't agree on what we wanted to do tonight, so we are ringing in the New Year each of us doing what we love to do," Harper reasoned.

Bullshit, I thought. There is no way I would spend New Year's Eve away from my boyfriend, especially one as handsome as Harper. There was definitely more to that story.

"Your turn," Harper quickly reminded me.

"I don't have a boyfriend or a date. I came with Stacey and Vivian to get out of the house tonight," I replied truthfully.

As soon as I heard the words come out of my mouth, the feelings I had tried to hide behind my smile for the entire evening came rushing back to me. I excused myself and left Harper at the table.

As I cried in the bathroom, I heard the countdown, *TEN, NINE, EIGHT, SEVEN, SIX . . . HAPPY NEW YEAR!*

For too many times to count, I had again subjected myself to yet another unhealthy relationship. And what's worse, I went in eyes wide open with Monty in spite of Stacey's words of caution and my own good judgment. In other words, he was literally a self-inflicted punishment, bright red, flashing warning lights included. At some point during my life's journey—exactly in between raising my children and establishing a career—it must have slipped my mind that I too deserved respect and appreciation.

Things had to get better soon.

∽

"What did you think of the set, sweetie?" Stacey asked me the following afternoon.

"I enjoyed it. I didn't know what to expect, but the atmosphere was really cool and everyone was pretty nice."

"I saw you dance with Harper and then you kind of disappeared for a while."

"Yeah, the emotions of the night just caught up with me, that's all," I explained.

"Well, at least you got out and had a good time. Did you get any other dances in?" Stacey asked, trying her best to avoid the subject of my temporary emotional breakdown.

"I was a nervous wreck, but both CJ and Cameron asked

me to dance. I danced once with John, too."

"Excellent," Stacey added. "Pretty soon there will be a line of guys waiting to get you on the dance floor."

Stacey was clearly more sure of that than I was.

"Now, when are you going to use your Christmas present and go to the spa? Bring my goddaughters over here and go get some pampering!" Stacey ordered.

Chapter Seven

It had been three weeks since I had been to class. Not only was I still pretty humiliated after my ridiculous disappearing act on New Year's Eve, but it also certainly didn't help that I had been avoiding Monty's daily calls, texts, and emails begging for forgiveness and asking for another chance.

"When are you coming back to class, Gigi?" Vivian asked.

"It's only been a few weeks, Viv," I reasoned. "I will be back."

"I know, but you will forget everything you learned so far!" She was really serious about this.

"Well, I have had to pull some late nights at work and have been busy with the kids since the holidays . . . Viv, Monty wants to see me again."

"You are full of shit, Gigi. I am tired of telling you that Monty was not good for you. You knew it long before you got the proof. I know that Stacey is all *nurturing* and trying to give you time, but screw him! Why are you letting him still have so much control over you? Face it, G, he was a no-good, rebound, temporary way to pass the time, good fuck gone wrong!"

Damn. And there you have it. I guess I had forgotten that there was an expiration date on feeling sorry for myself, but I could always count on Vivian to tell me exactly what I needed to hear, no matter how tough it was. Besides, I knew she was right.

"I will be back in class on Thursday, Ms. Vivian Monroe," I replied.

"Don't make me come and get you because you know I will."

"Yes, ma'am! I am saluting you over the phone."

"You know I love you, G, but he's not worth it," Vivian said in an uncharacteristically caring tone.

"I know. Thank you, Viv. And I do miss coming to class. What's been happening? I miss anything?"

Vivian told me that the last few weeks in class had been spent working on some advanced-level turns and giving the contest participants the opportunity to travel the perimeter of the floor. Apparently, the most effective way to show off competition savvy was to travel counterclockwise around the outer edge of the dance floor, similar to ballroom dancers, so that the judges would be sure to see every move. Vivian also told me that Dawn, the apparent leader of the Secret Seven, had asked about me. Spying already.

"I told her nosey ass that you were handling your business and that she should mind her own," Vivian snapped.

"You didn't have to be rude, Viv," I said. "You know how folks are."

"She didn't even know your name! She saw Harper asking me where you had been and then her nosey ass had to know too."

"Wait, you didn't tell me Harper asked about me," I said, a bit more interested now.

"Yep, he said he hadn't seen you since New Year's Eve and wondered if you were coming back. Hmm . . . bet your ass is coming back now, right?"

"I already said I was coming back. Remember—you threatened me about five minutes ago."

"Oh right," Vivian said with a chuckle.

∽

I made it back to class the following week. My beginner buddies, Eleana and Sasha, were a few turns ahead of me, but I was able to catch up pretty quickly. It was good to be back. Both CJ and Cam were there and flashed those perfect smiles welcoming me back to class. Neither Viv or Stacey made it this week, but I saw Harper across the room with his dance partner, Eva.

When class ended, CJ asked Cam to do a demonstration with me for the group. I was so nervous. Cam reassured me that I knew how to follow his signals, and he led me perfectly through a right turn, a left spin, and then a double right turn. That was the longest sixty seconds of my life. The class applauded my efforts and it was time to go home.

Since we were both beginners, I spent some time talking to Sasha about the classes I missed. We were chatting about the idea of going to some of the sets and other events coming up when Cam approached us.

"Excuse me, ladies. Gigi, I wanted to let you know that both CJ and I offer private lessons if you think you will miss classes. You seem to catch on pretty quickly, but I wanted you to know that privates are an option if you have other obligations during regular class time. That goes for you, too, Sasha. You ladies have a nice night."

Cam handed both Sasha and me his business card.

"Thanks, Cam," I said with a smile. "I will definitely keep that in mind."

"Wasn't that thoughtful?" Sasha said. "Girl, if I weren't happily married, which I am, I'd say he is one nice, tall drink of water!" We laughed.

I told Sasha to give me a ring when she got the courage to dance in public, and I would join her for moral support. We exchanged numbers and I headed for the door.

I felt a tug on my arm as I was walking to my car. Harper had caught up to me.

"So why did you just leave me at the table like that on New Year's Eve?" he asked.

"Well . . .," I stumbled, knowing that I did not have an explanation that I wanted to share, "hello to you too, Harper."

"Forgive me. That was rude. How are you doing, Gigi Grant?"

"I am well, thank you. Now to answer your question." I was glad that I had bought a little time to come up with something. "I always call my daughters at midnight to wish them a happy new year. I left the room because I knew I wouldn't be able to hear them over the phone if I stayed inside the set."

"Hmm." Harper smirked, clearly not believing my story. "Okay. Whatever the reason, the way I see it, you owe me part two of a conversation."

"Okay," I said, trying not to grin, "you name the place and time."

"Yes I will. Let me know when you will be in and around downtown and we can get together for tea," Harper said. "Here's my card. Hit me up and let me know your schedule."

"That sounds perfect," I happily agreed. "I will definitely let you know."

∽

It was a relatively warm late January afternoon in Minneapolis. The sun was shining and the wind was calm. Harper and I met at a small, completely charming tea bar on the edge of downtown. I had finished a rather successful client meeting nearby, so I was in a pretty good mood. After we greeted one another with a polite hug, we sat at a table near a window.

"Thanks for reaching out to let me know when you were available," Harper acknowledged. "I wasn't sure that you would."

"Why not?" I asked.

"Well, after that business I gave you about a girlfriend . . . let's just say I wasn't really at the top of my game on New Year's Eve."

"You should know that I don't too much care for games, Harper," I said with a smile, of course.

"Gotcha. Laying it on the line already, huh?" Harper smiled back.

I returned the smile and continued, "But now that you

have brought it up, why don't you tell me about this girl-friend?"

Harper explained that he had been in a relationship with a woman for about two years, but they were not "exclusive," whatever that meant. They met a few years after he moved to the Twin Cities while he was showing a condominium. As a real estate agent, he met lots of people, but this woman caught his eye because she knew exactly what she wanted in her home. No matter how he tried to tempt her with alternatives that were equally attractive, he was unable to close that sale until he found the size, location, and amenities that she simply had to have. He told me that he admired her tenacity.

Sure. I bet it was the tenacity that he admired.

On a more personal note, I learned that Harper hailed from Detroit, Michigan, and was the youngest child in a large family. He started stepping a little over three years ago as a social outlet. He had several close friends in the city but no family. He had never been married and had no children. I'm not sure if he meant to do so, but he actually admitted that he loved to be in the company of women. Well, in my opinion, that must have been at least one of the reasons he had been single for so long.

"I'm not encouraging you to join me on a second date, am I?" Harper asked.

"I didn't know this was a first date, Harper, but to answer your question, I have never backed down from a challenge."

He smiled as if he really liked my answer.

"Now it's your turn. You're a decorator, huh? Do you ever do any staging for real estate sales?"

All I could hear were Stacey's words in the back of my mind: "Be friendly enough to make business connections because you never know."

"I did some staging earlier in my career, but most of my current contracts are for corporate clients," I explained. "Doesn't mean I wouldn't consider it if the right opportunity came along."

"Cool," Harper added. "I have a listing that definitely needs a feminine touch. A complete bachelor pad right down to the futon and weight bench in the living room and the black lacquer headboard in the bedroom."

"You mean no George Foreman Grill on the countertop?" I asked.

"How did you know? I made him put that away for showings," Harper joked.

"But let's get back to you and me, Ms. Gigi Grant. You are all in my personal business asking questions about girlfriends and the like . . . how many guys are you seeing?"

"I beg your pardon, Harper." I pretended to be offended. "Are you somehow insinuating that I—"

"Wait, wait, stop, before this goes any further," Harper interrupted. "You are a very *beautiful* and *successful* woman. I am sure your dance card is full."

"Oh," I stumbled. "I am social, but nothing serious. Just worked my way out of something pretty destructive, so I'm taking it easy on myself for a while."

"Ahh, now your disappearance on New Year's Eve makes more sense," Harper sympathized, I think. "But maybe we should save that story for another time."

"Is that your subtle way of asking me to join you at another tea bar?" I shamelessly flirted.

"Maybe. Or maybe a real date next time," Harper said as he winked.

"We shall see, Mr. Drake. You have already confessed to enjoying being in the company of women, *plural*. So I think I get to ask you the same question. Mr. *Handsome* and *Successful*, how many women are you seeing?"

"Just because I enjoy the company of women doesn't mean that I indulge in that behavior. I will take someone out to a movie or for dinner, but I am very clear about expectations," Harper reassured.

"And are these women who step?" I decided to push a little further.

Harper chuckled. "I can honestly tell you that I have never called one of these steppers *my girl*. Too much drama and too little privacy."

"Hmm. What about your dance partner, Eva? I heard some dance partners are actually *partners*." I was exhibiting blatant nosiness at this point.

"Lesson number one in the stepping community: don't believe everything you hear, Gigi. Let me guess—Vivian?" he asked with a little something in his tone. "Eva and I are only dance partners. No more. No less. It's all about the dance, at least for me, and hopefully for her too. Besides that, I am pretty sure she has a man in her life. I don't know her well, but she is getting pretty good and we dance together a lot. Other than that, I think she is cool. Listen, Gigi, I haven't met anyone who steps that I could get serious about."

"Hey, you don't owe me any explanations. This is only tea!" I reasoned. "Besides, we have already established the fact that you have a *tenacious* girlfriend."

"That is correct. But I have also told you that we both see other people. And when I think that person will be really special, I bring her to my favorite tea bar," he said with another wink.

There was that smile again.

"I'll let you get away with that for now." I smiled back.

After about another hour of casual conversation, we finished our tea and stood to exit the bar. Harper extended his arm and walked me to my car. We leaned against my door like a couple of teenagers. Glad the car was clean for a change.

"By the way, Gigi, is that your real name?"

"No, my first name is actually Gabrielle. Gabrielle Grant—GG. It evolved into Gigi over time, since about fifth grade. I was Gabby up until then."

"Well, I don't like it."

"Excuse me?" I said with a frown.

"No, I just mean I don't want to call you by the same name that everyone else calls you. Too impersonal. What's your middle name?"

"Would you believe Ginger? Turns out that my mom was a fan of Tina Louise, the actress who played the actress on *Gilligan's Island*. Remember Ginger Grant?" I painfully admitted.

"Wow," Harper said with a raised brow. "So, Miss Gabrielle Ginger Grant, what shall it be? Gabby? Nah.

Gabrielle? Maybe. Three-G?"

"Hell no!"

We both laughed.

"Mind if I call you Ginger? It's a cool name, and it definitely suits you. I think your mother knew exactly what she was doing."

Wow, what a cute smile he had. "I am okay with that, Mr. Drake."

"Groovy."

Like a perfect gentleman, Harper opened my car door and closed it after I was inside. He motioned for me to lower the window.

"I had a good time, Ginger. I look forward to hearing more of your story."

He leaned in and kissed me on the cheek.

"Thanks for the smiles, Harper. See you in class."

∽

Over the next several weeks, Harper and I met a few times for tea and we went to dinner once after he showed me the bachelor pad he had asked me to stage for him. I was beginning to really enjoy his company. We definitely spent time talking about business, but I found that he was easy to talk to about other things, as well. Politics, social welfare, family, and even religion. We didn't always agree, but we certainly respected one anothers' opinions. Of course, with the competition only a few short weeks away, we talked about dancing, too.

I had been traveling a bit on business and missed a few classes in January and February, but Harper had been kind enough to squeeze in a few private lessons for me in between his practices with Eva. I was still a total beginner, but I always felt like I was somehow doing better when I danced with Harper.

"So, are you ready for the big weekend? It will be exciting for you to see your first stepping contest. Steppers from all over the Midwest and beyond will be asking you to dance," Harper teased.

"That is not funny. I am so not ready for that," I replied, almost sick to my stomach.

"You are more ready than you think. I dance with you enough to know that you can catch all the basic moves and more. Besides, these cats out here are just trying to get their arms around a pretty girl. Don't worry too much about missing a step."

"Really? Is that it? Are we back in high school? As long as I look pretty and smile, it doesn't matter what my feet are doing?" I asked, almost appalled by Harper's statement.

"You got it, Ginger!" Harper was cracking himself up. "But seriously," he said as he tried to gather his composure, "your dance is fine for a beginning stepper. Better than fine. And I don't have to tell you that you are a knockout, so I will be the one waiting in line for a dance with you."

"Whatever, Harper. You will never have to wait in line for a dance with me."

Damn! I said that out loud. Too late.

"I mean, I would never keep my favorite instructor waiting." I tried to recover.

"That is sweet, but you will see. I guarantee it. But on that subject, Ms. Grant, I am really going to have to get in some practice time with Eva over the next few weeks so that we are ready. Do you mind if we pick up where we left off with your lessons a few weeks after the contest? Well, if you want to continue, I mean. I will definitely need to take a break for a few weeks once it's over."

"Of course," I tried to answer in my most sincere voice. "That makes perfect sense. Eva is a great dancer. How did you two become partners?"

"CJ always pairs me up with someone for the competition. Eva has a salsa dance background and is a good dancer, but fundamentally speaking, she is still a beginning stepper. I think we will do all right if I am able to . . ."

"Able to what?" I wanted him to finish his sentence.

"I just have to be a little more patient and put the dance first. This is not my first contest and there are a lot of politics, emotions, and bullshit as with any other business. When it's all said and done, none of those things matter to me. I dance because I enjoy it and because it makes me feel as though I am a part of something bigger than myself. A community. History."

I think I was beginning to understand what Harper meant by that.

"Okay, Mr. Drake. I wish you and Eva good luck, and I will save a number on my dance card for you," I said with a big smile.

"Wow, you have a beautiful smile, Gabrielle Ginger Grant, and I *will* find you for that dance."

∞ *Chapter Eight*

The big steppers' weekend had arrived. The first two nights included meet-and-greet events with out-of-town steppers, bowling and pizza parties, and a few other activities arranged on a smaller scale. But it was finally Saturday night: the night of the main event, the big contest. Both Vivian and Stacey were working with the Untouchable Steppers team behind the scenes to help CJ and Cam pull everything together. Sasha and I were already staying in the host hotel, so we planned to meet in my room and head down to the ballroom early to make sure we had good seats at the Minnesota tables.

When the elevator doors opened, it was as if we had stepped out into another world. The otherwise ordinary hallway on the second floor of the Marriott hotel had been transformed into a stepping extravaganza. There were things and people everywhere. A few contestants practicing some moves in one corner. Another couple having a heated argument in another corner. But the most noticeable attraction of all was the arcade of vendors peddling their wares. Tables and tables of steppers from across the country selling their specialty merchandise. I mean, there were hats, jewelry, scarves, artwork, clothing, shoes, CDs, T-shirts, handbags—you name it, you could buy it. So much to look at and so many choices to make. From the first table to the last, if you were unhappy with your outfit, you could have an entirely new one, from head to toe, by the time you reached the ballroom door. That included accessories and even a weave if you were having a bad hair day. And here I thought entrepreneurship was all the rage among Minnesota steppers. Apparently it was a nationwide phenomenon. I was quickly beginning to realize that this whole stepping thing was a business indeed.

As we continued our journey down the crowded hallway to the main ballroom, we passed the hospitality suite where most of the contestants were hanging out and receiving contest logistics from CJ. Just then, I saw Harper from behind, talking to another contestant. I hadn't seen him for a few weeks, but we had exchanged a number of text messages and phone calls. As we caught up to him, he turned around just as I was about to tap him on the shoulder.

"Hey, Ginger, you look beautiful tonight," Harper said with a big smile before he kissed me on the cheek.

"Thanks, Harper. You look terribly handsome. Hey, have you met Sasha? She started taking classes the same time as I did."

"No, not officially. Nice to meet you, Sasha," Harper said, bowing slightly and shaking Sasha's hand.

"Nice to meet you too," Sasha replied with a grin.

"Gotta run and get our contestant number. See you inside," Harper said as he hurried away.

"Okay, good luck!" I said.

"Hey! Don't forget to save me that dance," he shouted with a wink as he rushed toward the contestant room.

"Well, he seemed nice," Sasha teased. "And who is Ginger?"

"Inside joke," I said, trying to change the subject. "Let's grab our seats!"

Sasha and I had prepurchased our tickets so we didn't have to stand in the tremendous line that had formed immediately outside of the ballroom.

"Hey, Gigi!" I heard Stacey shout from behind the long line of patrons waiting to purchase tickets. "Find me before the contest is over. I need to tell you something!"

"Okay," I answered with a wave of my hand.

CJ and Cam had tables reserved and designated for their students and other locals they had invited to attend the event. The theme of the night was "Steppin' in Purple," so the room was filled with balloons, streamers, and other decor in every shade. There was a purple hue to the room as if all the lightbulbs had been changed to the color of lavender. I wore a dark purple dress with a purple flower in my hair. Sasha wore a black and purple pants suit with a purple hat. Everyone looked beautiful.

Right away, I noticed the room was divided by city. There was a group of tables for the Twin Cities, of course, then groups of tables for Chicago, Indianapolis, one for Milwaukee, and then a smaller area of tables for other visitors from New York, Arizona, Iowa, and Nebraska. A large group of line dancers had taken command of the floor. The giant purplish mass was downright entertaining as they moved in unison to something called the Bikers' Shuffle. This group was definitely having a fabulous time on the dance floor. And as I looked more closely, they also appeared to be pretty exhausted as they headed back to their tables at the end of the song. Within a few minutes of taking our seats, CJ and Cam were onstage welcoming everyone to the Twin Cities and thanking guests for traveling to join Untouchable Steppers for its annual event: US vs. Them.

"Before we get on with the main event, we have a special treat tonight," CJ started. "Let's put our hands together for our very own Ivy Prince and her line dancers of DDD, Dynamic Divas of Dance!"

The crowd was on its feet in applause. I had seen a few line dances during the New Year's Eve set I attended, but I had never been to Ivy's line dance class. Clearly I was missing out on something big.

Just as CJ left the stage, there were pink spotlights amid the purple. Ivy sauntered out onto the dance floor followed by four line dancers from her class. They were wearing black dresses, pink belts and scarves, and of course, pink high heel shoes. The ladies performed a sexy line dance routine to three popular R&B songs. If you didn't know they were the best of the best, they were letting you know tonight. The choreography was absolutely flawless and synchronized, and the crowd was going crazy with cheers. Not only that, but it looked like they were having fun. Maybe I would check out a line dance class one of these days.

After Ivy and her entourage had made their exit, Cam and CJ were back onstage.

"That Ivy sure knows how to put on a show, doesn't she, fellas?" Cam said with a wide grin. "Now let's get it started."

Suddenly the house lights were up. The soft purple hue

of the room vanished and was replaced by cold, unnerving spotlights filled with judgment, anxiety, and apprehension.

CJ chimed in. "Just as in years past, each of our out-of-town couples will share the dance floor with each of our Minnesota couples for about four minutes. We have six rounds this year. The highest scoring couples from each group will compete against one another for first and second place."

"Let's make sure to show our support," Cam continued. "It's not easy to get out there and do this, so if you see something you like, let them know it! Everybody, good luck and have fun! Let's go to work, steppers!"

Two by two, the couples made their way to the dance floor. Each couple sported coordinated outfits. Some were simple with complementary colors. Others actually had taken the time to make matching costumes. For about four minutes, couples did their fanciest footwork, turns, and spins, and then their opportunity to impress the judges was over. I saw Harper and Eva sitting near John and his dance partner from CJ's and Cam's class. I recognized the faces of only a few of the other Minnesota couples, but I really didn't know them any better than the out-of-town contestants.

After about twenty minutes, round four was about to begin. When the next two couples stood up to take their places on the floor, there was a soft chant coming from a few of the tables in the Chicago section of the ballroom. What were they saying?

"Kryptonite! Kryptonite! Kryptonite!"

As in *Superman*? Kryptonite? Who was this guy?

Well, no sooner than I asked that question to myself did

he hit the floor like a cyclone. Spinning effortlessly with controlled doubles, triples, quadruples—I stopped counting. His dance partner was perfectly poised and handled his moves and signals as if they had been dancing together since the time each of them could walk. They displayed flawlessly coordinated footwork and spins. At one point, I thought he was actually going to do the splits, but it turned out he was just taking a twirl on his knee. She wore a flowing gold and white gown to match his white tuxedo with tails trimmed in gold. Oh, can't forget the gold top hat.

Who in their right mind would want to follow that performance? I don't think anyone even noticed the Minnesota couple dancing on the floor at the same time as those two. Everything afterward would surely pale in comparison.

"Give them some love," Cam shouted from the stage as the couples following this Kryptonite guy reluctantly took their places on the dance floor. The crowd was polite with applause but noticeably quiet, as if they were still recovering from the excitement of the last round. Round five was pretty uneventful, and then it was over. It was finally round six, the last round of the night, and Harper and Eva were up.

As they took the floor, they both looked so serious. Where was that fabulous smile of his? The music started and they were off. They did a perfectly respectable dance and effortlessly traveled the perimeter of the floor, incorporating some impressive footwork and advanced turns. Their moves were so smooth and perfectly in sync. In my humble, unbiased, beginner stepper's opinion, I thought their dance definitely surpassed the performance of the couple from Milwaukee that took the floor with them. That Milwaukee male step-per tripped at least once, and his female counterpart literally had to run a few times to catch up to him on the dance floor.

"All right, all right, all right!" CJ was back on the micro-phone. "Let's give it up one more time for all of our perfor-mances tonight!"

The crowd stood to its feet to again applaud all of the contestants of the evening.

"Our team of counters have taken the tally sheets from the judges and are in the process of totaling scores. We have about fifteen minutes before we announce our winners, so let's get some music playing." CJ motioned to the DJ.

Sasha and I were huddled up, talking about everything we had just seen. We couldn't help but marvel at the skill of some of the dancers, and the outfits! As I looked around the room, I saw a few dancers had taken the floor, but most people were in clusters, clearly having discussions about the contest and making their own decisions about who should be crowned victor. Sasha and I were looking to ask anyone who might know about this Kryptonite guy when we heard CJ back onstage.

"Okay, everyone. Attention please. We have the first-round winners," CJ proclaimed. "From Minnesota, our top scores belong to Rocco and Lena, and from out-of-town, our Chicago steppers, Kurt and Janet!"

The crowd cheered as the two couples took the floor for the final round. Apparently Mr. Kryptonite's government name was Kurt.

I didn't recognize Rocco and Lena and had never seen

them in CJ's and Cam's classes. I did remember their black and white outfits and thought they had done a nice job during the first round.

As everyone expected, Mr. Kryptonite turned it up a level and performed like the master stepper that he so obviously represented. Rocco and Lena held their own as well, playing more to the lighter side of the dance by incorporating romantic, close moves that left no one to question their connection both on and off the dance floor. I suppose they figured there was no point competing against the showstopping whirlwind that was Kurt, so they performed to their strengths. Even though I had never seen them before, their playfulness and charisma were undeniable, and they were a fun couple to watch.

When the dance ended, everyone waited patiently for the final vote. CJ took the stage a few minutes later.

"With a lead of eighteen points, for the second year in a row, Kurt and Janet are the first-place winners of tonight's competition!"

As the crowd continued to cheer, the first- and second-place winners received their trophies and cash while lots of photos were taken. CJ and Cam thanked the judges, DJs, and photographers, as well as the team of US steppers that helped them pull everything together. A few seconds later, the lights went back down and the room was all purple again. It was time for the rest of us to dance.

Sasha and I were soon approached by a pair of incredibly short men. I am five feet three and Sasha is a few inches taller than I am. I had on an average-sized heel, but they were undeniably short. In fact, as I looked around the room, there were quite a few short men in attendance. Interesting. I wondered if there was a story there. And wait a minute, had I been remiss in mentioning the fact that all of these steppers were very mature? *Very* mature, well into their forties, fifties, and sixties. Yes, sixties.

But I digress. The two suitors who approached Sasha and me were not twins, but they were certainly related. They introduced themselves as steppers from Arizona. We politely took their hands and they led us to the dance floor. I flashed a nervous smile Sasha's way as she tossed a pair of crossed fingers in the air for good luck.

It wasn't so bad. I had only danced with four different people over the last four months, so it was an interesting experience. It didn't take long for my Arizonian partner to figure out that I was a beginner.

"How long have you been dancing?" he asked.

"About four months. Is it that obvious?" I replied.

"No, no, nothing like that," he answered. "My brother and I are instructors in Phoenix, so I know a beginner when I dance with one. You are doing very well for a four-month-old stepper," he said with a grin.

When the song was over, he walked me back to my seat and handed me his business card.

"Look us up if you are ever in Phoenix," he said as he kissed the top of my hand.

"Sure. Thanks for the dance," I replied.

I thought for a second that there must be a guidebook called *Gentleman's Etiquette for Stepping*. All the men appeared to be so polite and patient when taking your hand for a dance. It was refreshing to be in a room filled with grown folks' behavior.

As my Phoenix dance partner walked away, Stacey was again motioning me toward her from across the room, almost feverishly this time. Each time I started walking her way, it seemed as though I was intercepted and ended up back on the dance floor.

After my third dance of the night, I saw Harper walking toward me. He had untied his bowtie, removed his jacket, and rolled up his sleeves. He looked a little defeated, but he still had a smile on his face. He was just a few short feet away when a handsome stranger stretched out his hand and asked me to dance. As much as I wanted to push him aside and say, "Can't you see Harper coming to ask me to dance?" I graciously agreed and we headed to the dance floor. Harper took Sasha's hand instead.

"How are you feeling tonight, Gigi? I've been waiting for a chance to connect with you all night long."

What the hell? Who was this dude? Oh no, oh no, oh no. I had been so mesmerized by the atmosphere of the evening that my Spidey-senses were not on point. Now I realized in the worst possible way why Stacey had been trying to grab my attention all night. Although I was just learning the dance, I was not a complete virgin to the stepping scene, literally.

Two summers ago I had visited Stacey in Charlotte and she had taken me to my very first steppers' set. Emotionally and financially speaking, I was not in an ideal place. Work was really slow and I wasn't receiving a penny in the way of financial support from my daughters' father, so I had to secure a loan to keep us afloat. My stepfather passed away in early summer, so I had spent some time with my mother to make sure she had all of her business affairs in order. And, of course, I was in the process of decompressing after ending yet another failed relationship. With things a mess at home, I decided to hang out with my bestie for a few weeks in her new town. Stacey had only been dancing a year at that time, but she insisted that we check out a steppers' set hosted by the instructor of the class she had been attending for the last few months since moving to Charlotte. When we arrived at the set held in a ballroom of the Charlotte Westin, I remember thinking, *What a grown-up atmosphere.* I was in awe as I watched couples move in what appeared to be seamless ribbons across the dance floor. Even though Stacey was relatively new to the dance, she was certainly not shy and did not stay in her seat for very long. I met a few steppers who were happy to share a dance with me—among other things—even though I had no idea what I was doing. It turned out to be an enjoyable experience and an easy way to escape in a discreet "I will never see you again" sort of fashion. So I thought.

"So how have you been?" the Charlotte stranger asked.

"Good, good," I said. I was a flustered mess at this point.

"You do remember me, don't you?" he asked.

"Of course," I said with a forced smile. "I met you in Charlotte a few years ago when I could barely count to eight on the dance floor."

He grinned, showing all of his teeth. Almost like a wolf.

"Well, I see you are getting the hang of it now. Are you taking class with CJ and Cam?"

Oh no, had he already shared my business with the twins?

"Yes," I answered, "and a few private lessons."

"Cool. I can give you one tonight if you want," the stranger said as he pulled me close, even though it was not that kind of song.

The song, which was apparently the longest stepping track on the face of the planet, was finally ending. Peeking over the shoulder of my dance partner, I could see Harper walk Sasha back to her seat. The Charlotte stranger appeared to have no intention of ending our dance just yet. I wondered if Harper caught a glimpse of my distress as he casually walked toward us and tapped my stranger on the shoulder.

"Hey, brother, mind if I cut in? Gigi here promised me a dance if I didn't win the contest tonight, and I am on my way out the door."

The stranger turned around, "Oh sure, man. I don't blame you—she looks gorgeous tonight. Hey, G," he continued, "I will give you a buzz before I head back to Charlotte."

"Okay," I said as I politely waved to him.

"You okay?" Harper asked as we started to dance.

"I am now. Thanks for the rescue," I said.

When we finished our dance, Harper escorted me back to my seat and whispered in my ear, "Text me your room number." Then he walked away.

It took me a minute, literally sixty seconds, to decide whether or not to do it. Naturally, I began to reason with myself. Harper and I are just friends, right? Besides, I hadn't seen him for a few weeks since our last private lesson and I did want to talk to him about the competition, especially this Kryptonite guy. It didn't take me long at all to convince myself that I should invite him to my room.

On our way to the elevators, Sasha and I ran into Cam in the hallway and thanked him for a great weekend of events.

"Tell CJ we had a good time too!" Sasha added.

"Will do, ladies. See you in class," Cam replied.

About an hour after I sent Harper the text with my room number, I received a reply: "On my way up." I had been talking to Sasha, who was still excited from the evening. After we ended our call, I barely had enough time to get out of that purple dress and slip into my pajamas, which were way less than sexy. It was nearly two o'clock in the morning and I had just opened a bottle of wine so that I wouldn't have to take it back home with me later in the day.

Just then I heard a single knock at the door.

"Hey you," I said as I opened the door.

"Wow, you look cute in your PJs," Harper said with a smile.

"Whatever, Harper Drake. What's going on?"

I could barely finish my question before Harper put his arms around my waist and kissed me. Nice, he had only kissed me on the cheek up until now.

"I needed that," he said.

"I repeat—what's going on?" I asked again.

"It was a long evening. The tensions and stress were high, and I am sooooo glad that it's over," he said.

"I thought you guys did great! No screw-ups . . . unlike that couple from Milwaukee." The smirk on Harper's face told me that he agreed.

"Our dance was ordinary. There was no chemistry. It was almost like I was dancing with a complete stranger."

"Was she nervous?" I wondered.

"Maybe, but I don't think so. I was concerned about dancing with a partner that I hadn't developed a real connection with. Stepping is a *couples* dance—even more so for competitive purposes. We had practiced so much over the last few weeks that I thought we were going to be okay. But what's worse is that Eva had been fighting with her man for the last few days, and then when he didn't show up to support her tonight, she could barely focus. She was distracted and didn't catch a few of my signals."

"Well, I don't think anyone noticed," I reassured him.

"I noticed."

"How about a glass of wine," I offered.

"Sure."

As I poured his glass of wine, I told Harper to make himself comfortable. He tossed his suitcoat onto the chair, removed his bow tie, and began to unbutton his shirt. He hopped onto the bed to take off his shoes, and I sat down beside him. I handed him the glass of wine and unfastened his shirt the rest of the way.

Damn he smells good.

"Wow, you smell nice, Ginger," Harper said.

Oh my, was he reading my thoughts now?

"By the way, who was that guy groping you on the dance

floor?" Harper asked me with a chuckle.

"Let's just call him . . . an indiscretion gone wrong. Thanks again for pulling me away from that one," I replied. "I didn't realize that steppers make up such a small world."

"Got that right—you never know who you might run into at a set. I bet money he was trying to get up to this room," Harper said with a raised brow.

Boy was he ever. Good thing my phone was on silent. I had already deleted four text messages and ignored two phone calls from my Charlotte stranger.

"No chance of that," I said. "I have exactly who I want in this room tonight."

He flashed that gorgeous smile and placed his hand on mine.

"Now that we have that settled," I decided, "tell me, who in the hell is this Kurt Kryptonite?"

Harper told me that Kurt Kryptonite, known to ordinary folk as Kurt Curtis, was a master stepper who lived and breathed the dance in Chicago. He was a childhood friend of the twins and started stepping the same time as the brothers. Kurt and the brothers had grown up together and attended the same high school, but when the twins went off to college, Kurt remained in Chicago, working in a high-paying manufacturing job. When CJ retired from football and the boys returned home after their parents had passed, they reconnected with Kurt and all had decided to learn this new style of stepping, the eight count. Now anyone who had seen Kurt dance knew that he had excelled at the dance. But somewhere along the line, it created a division between him and the twins. Can't you picture it? "This town ain't big enough for three master steppers." Well, instead of having a series of old-fashioned Western shootouts, the great city of Chicago became a segmented and territorial metropolis with clear lines of division in the stepping community. The brothers moved to the Twin Cites shortly thereafter, and their nemesis, Kurt, along with many other self-proclaimed master steppers, remained in Chicago.

"Rumor has it that Kurt travels around the country competing in small local competitions for easy money."

"I don't get it. What's the point?" I asked.

"As you saw tonight, Kurt is a great dancer. For that reason, he could probably win just about any contest. So the story goes, he purposely avoids participating in the larger national contests because winning one of those could disqualify him from competing in the smaller local competitions," Harper explained.

Kurt knew that his reputation preceeded him, so not only did he come to town once in a while to rattle the brothers, take their money, and dominate contests, but he was sure to capitalize on his visits by offering profitable workshops and private lessons to allegedly share his techniques and philosophy behind the dance.

"Would you believe that I have heard that this guy actually offers memberships to his stepping organization?" Harper continued. "Last figure I heard was three thousand dollars in annual dues to become a charter member of Krytonite Steppers, Ltd.!"

"Wow," I said, looking puzzled. "Really? I had no idea that people would pay that kind of money to learn a dance."

"Oh, you would be surprised," Harper added. "The crazy thing is that no matter how many lessons, classes, workshops, or charter memberships in which you participate, you are still going to dance like YOU! But, hey, business is business. Gotta admire the brother for doing his thing and doing it like no other."

"But why *Kryptonite*?" I asked.

Harper could barely answer through his amusement.

"Well, I suppose Kurt is to stepping what Krytonite is to Superman . . . invincible."

We both chuckled this time.

When I asked about why I had never seen Rocco and Lena, the couple that won first place on the local front, Harper explained that they were students of another instructor in town.

"Yeah, Rocco is cool. His wife, Lena, seems to be cool too. This brother, named Link, teaches a class across the river in St. Paul, and those two are his claim to fame. They have been dancing together since a time before I started. Link has sets too, in the cities. I am sure that you will attend one of his parties sooner or later. In fact, I know that one is coming up in a few months. I will keep you posted because I will be interested to hear what you think."

"Okay. Well, I really enjoyed watching those two. Even though the tornado was on the floor at the same time, he was not able to completely distract me from giving them some attention."

"That's why they are the couple to beat," Harper said. "When partners are truly connected, the relationship between the two of them is completely apparent on the dance floor."

"Interesting," I said.

"And true," Harper added, as if he were speaking from personal experience.

"Uh-huh," I started, "let's hear it."

"Nothing to tell," Harper said. "A little over a year ago, I had another dance partner, Alex, and we were pretty close. We danced well together, and we definitely had a connection."

"Did you win?" I asked.

"No," Harper said in a defeated tone. "I realized very quickly that connection and charisma go right out the window when drama sets in. She was way too much drama."

"Is that why you stopped being partners?" I asked.

"That is mostly the reason," Harper said, "but she moved to California almost immediately after our competition. In fact, she was actually here tonight."

"Oh," I said, "you didn't get invited to her room?" I teased with a big fake grin.

"Nope! Even if I had, there's no way I would bring that back into my life. Besides, I am sure she has plenty of attention from the opposite sex. Just like you did tonight! Yep, that's right! I saw you going to work," he said. "Those brothers were all over you! Told you your dance card would be full."

Harper paused a moment and looked at me seriously.

"Ginger, ever think you might participate in a contest?"

"What?" I asked, completely astounded. "I don't know. I can't imagine ever competing with some of those fabulous dancers."

As we sipped our second and third glasses of wine, I told Harper that I had been missing my private lessons with him and that I still needed to learn that dip that he tried in class almost three months ago now.

"Then let's do it . . . right now until we have perfected it," he said in a professorial tone. "You see, the *dip* is very personal and varies depending on the two who are dancing together, so no two dips are ever the same."

He was so silly I could hardly stop giggling. Not to mention the fact that we were both completely deprived of sleep and tipsy from too much wine. Nevertheless, Harper proceeded to dip me again, and again, and again until we got it right . . . for us. We were laughing so hard by dip number six that we both landed on the floor. He stood, helped me to my feet, and told me he should probably head home.

"Check this out, Ginger, the sun is up and it is almost seven o'clock," Harper noticed. "I kept you up all night. Let me get out of here."

"You gonna make it home okay?"

"Of course. I can't believe we talked all night long. Thank you for listening and for sharing more of you with me. For someone I only met a few short months ago, I am really beginning to enjoy what I hear."

"See you soon?"

"Maybe not on the dance floor, but definitely soon. Like I told you after our last lesson together, I definitely need a break from stepping for a hot minute. But I will hit you up soon for sure. I will be expecting you to catch that dip next time we dance."

Harper gave me a big hug and kiss before he left. I closed the hotel room door behind him and immediately called for a late checkout. It had been a great night, but I needed a few hours of shut-eye.

❧ Chapter Nine

I had been traveling quite a bit—back-to-back trips within a three-week period. Building an interior decorating clientele out of state was tiresome and time consuming, to say the least. But when friends in high places recommended me, I didn't mind a complimentary trip to New York or Los Angeles every now and again to consult with a potential new client. I missed my girls when I was gone, but they were always in very capable hands with our favorite caregiver, Heidi.

I made it back to my hotel room after a client dinner. I was about to call Isabel and Grace to say good night when I saw Stacey's name pop up on my phone screen.

"How's the new business coming, Gigi? Any commitments yet?"

"Getting close," I said. "What's going on at home?"

"Not much. Greg and the kids are good. The girls with Heidi?"

"You know it," I responded. "Hey, have you been to class?"

"I made it once in the last few weeks, but I've had a few board meetings lately that have been conflicting with the class schedule."

"I feel like I am missing so much. I haven't been to class since the week before the steppers' contest—that was over three weeks ago!" I told her. "And even though I am back home next week, I will miss class to attend Isabel's choir concert."

"That's right. With both of us in and out of town for the last three weeks, I haven't talked to you since the contest. How did you handle Mr. Charlotte when he finally caught up to you?"

"Oh my goodness. It was awkward to say the least, but disaster was averted when Harper stepped in."

Stacey paused a minute.

"Have you given any thought to asking the twins about a private lesson?" she asked.

"You know what—I hadn't really considered it because I had been getting a little one-on-one time with Harper," I accidentally admitted.

"Ooh, I see," Stacey said. "That's the second time I have heard the name Harper in the last five minutes. What's going on with you two?"

"You know, we hang out and have good talks. Our businesses intersect, and we can talk about the real estate market and staging and sales, all that fun stuff. But we have also had some good talks about personal things, too. Besides, he has a girlfriend, Stace. Anyway, he seems to be a good guy, definitely a great dancer, and I like spending time with him, that's all."

"Uh-huh," Stacey muttered.

"What is that supposed to mean?" I asked.

"Oh nothing. So, what's the problem? Just get another lesson from Harper," Stacey concluded.

"He's taking a break from stepping for a minute. Last we talked—in person—he told me that he always takes a bit of a break after the contest," I told her.

"You haven't talked to Harper since the contest? That was over three weeks ago."

"We have talked on the phone and we text a little, but I haven't seen him."

"Then give one of the brothers a ring. I'm sure they will have some time to get you caught up. CJ told me that you are catching on pretty quickly."

"Maybe I will do that. Enough about class, girl. What's the latest in the world of public relations? Any juicy, illicit celebrity gossip you can share with your bestie?"

∽

"I am really glad you called me for a lesson," Cam said while he gave me a hello hug. "I was beginning to think you had given up on us."

Cam was able to meet me at the community center where classes were ordinarily held.

"Work travel has been keeping me so busy lately that I have missed almost a month of classes now," I said guiltily. "I remembered your offer and I left messages for both you and CJ, but you were the first to return my call."

"Whatever the reason, like I said, I am glad you called," Cam remarked. "Now let's see. Where did you leave off in your last class? Were you working on your left spin?"

For the next half hour, Cam drilled me on the turns I had

learned so far and reinforced the foundation and technical aspects of the dance. He taught me how to shift my weight to prepare for a properly given signal for a left spin and reminded me to stay on the balls of my feet or my toes at all times. We practiced lane control, and Cam emphasized the importance of being aware of sometimes severely limited space on the dance floor. Although the male leads the dance with his signals, those signals are given within the confines of an imaginary north–south "lane" he creates for his partner so that the flow of their steps can be maintained even in small spaces.

"Yeah, some dudes just go for it no matter how small the space might be," Cam explained. "We have been working with Michael for a few years now, but he's decided that he's gonna do him regardless of his surroundings and everybody else just better watch out."

"Really?" I asked. "Well, if you are all over the place, won't you bump into people?"

"Yes," Cam said, totally frustrated and rolling his eyes.

"But enough about that, Gigi," Cam continued. "For someone who's only had a few months' worth of classes, you are getting the hang of this pretty quickly."

"I have a tiny confession," I started. "I have had a few private lessons with Harper—about a month ago when my schedule had once again been crazy."

"Oh—you and Harp, huh?" Cam smiled. "I can see that."

"I don't get what you mean," I said.

"I don't mean anything really. You are a pretty classy chick.

You carry yourself well. Harp is pretty quiet and private, so I could see why you two might vibe with one another."

"Thanks, I think. Harper and I are only dancing," I replied, seeing no need to tell him anything other than that.

"Famous last words!" Cam laughed. "Anyway, I've got you now, so let's see if we can get that dance to the next level."

By the time our lesson ended, both Cam and I had come out of our long sleeves and were sweating pretty good. I felt as though I had about five classes all at once, but it was good. I was all caught up and a little bit ahead of my peers as Cam taught me the extended right turn which, I think, would be tough to pick up in a classroom setting. We spent the next twenty minutes or so catching our breath, drinking water, and talking.

"So I know you and CJ are originally from Chicago. How often do you go back?" I asked.

"Since our folks passed, maybe about three times a year. We only go back to visit the old neighborhood and always to pick up a few new pieces of the dance to share in classes here."

"I've heard that there's lots of competition to be the best in Chicago," I said.

"I think there is room for everyone because each person brings something different to the dance. No two steppers look the same and *that* is what is so special and unique about it. Unfortunately, ignorance can cloud judgment, and people think they have a territory or some type of ownership of the dance. No one *owns* stepping, and no one can tell you that you're doing it wrong just because you're not doing it their way. Always remember that, Gigi," Cam said with some conviction.

Interesting, I thought.

"That's where CJ and I have the most conflict," Cam continued.

Finally I was gonna hear the good stuff.

"He really does believe that there is only one way to do this dance. He goes a little bit nuts when I tell our students there are variations and encourage them to make the dance their own. That's the only way anyone will be successful at it."

"That must be the reason you look like you are one with the music on the dance floor," I added. "I swear I can't tell where the dance floor ends and your feet begin."

Cam flashed a blushing smile.

"It's all about the music for me. The fundamentals are critical, no doubt. But when it's all said and done, you have to be able to feel how the music is telling you to move. *That* is the moment when your dance becomes yours, and *that* cannot be taught."

"Wow, that is definitely something to think about," I said.

"When you step," Cam continued, "it opens you up to a world of style, grace, and individualized beauty. It becomes a way of life right before your very eyes. And then, once you fall in love with stepping, it just might help you find that piece of yourself that you didn't even know was missing."

Cam was so passionate. His words and expression were so heartfelt and genuine, as though he were speaking from personal experience. I found myself totally speechless. Then he smiled.

"Of course it is not without its fair share of drama and silliness, but you get my meaning. You're on your way, Gigi. Good class today. Listen, you keep dancing with Harp, but if he can't fit you in, I am happy to keep working with you too."

"Thanks, Cam. It was fun."

I paid Cam for class and gave him a big hug before heading to my car. As I passed the window, I noticed that he had started to dance again. I paused just for a minute to watch him glide across the floor.

∞

After leaving my lesson with Cam, I headed to Vivian's to pick up the girls, who were getting their hair done.

"You had a private with *Cam*?" Vivian sounded confused.

"Well, yeah. He mentioned that was an option if I was going to miss some classes. You know I have been on the road for work, then Grace had that choir concert last week," I explained. "I called CJ, too, but Cam got back to me first."

"Oh."

"What's the matter, Viv?" I asked, hearing some kind of something in her tone.

"I have asked that damn Cameron for private lessons at least three times and he never gives me a date and time!"

"Oh" was all I could muster as a reply.

"Oh my ass!" Vivian shouted.

"Well don't get mad at me! Let me ask you this, crazy woman, have you made it clear that you only want to *dance* in these private lessons?"

"What are you implying, Gigi?"

"I ain't *implying* anything, Viv. I know your ass. Did you hit on Cam?"

"All I did was say that maybe we could get a drink after a private lesson at my house," Vivian clarified.

"Well, no wonder! He's probably afraid of you getting him alone!" I was cracking up with laughter.

"Whatever, Gigi." Vivian started to snicker, "I can't help it. That man is F-I-N-E!"

Vivian was nuts.

"Seriously though, girl, I need to talk to you about something, so call me when you get home and get settled."

"Will do," I assured Vivian.

∽

I called Vivian a few hours later, after making dinner for the girls and helping with homework due on Monday.

"What's up, girl?" I asked. "You sounded so serious earlier."

"Gigi, you know DJ Cool who deejays most of our sets? He comes to class sometimes too . . .," Vivian started.

"Yeah, I think so. Tall, darker complexion, kinda chubby?"

"That's muscle, G!" Vivian yelled.

"Okay, if you say so, Viv," I agreed in protest.

"Anyway, he called me up and asked me out."

"Okay. Hmm. I believe you were the very first person to tell me not to date any of these steppers," I quickly reminded Vivian of her own advice.

"I knew you were gonna say that," Vivian admitted.

"Of course," I said.

"Well, he's not exactly a stepper. He's a DJ," Vivian rationalized.

"But he dances. Same crowd, no difference," I opined. "Why are we even going through this debate? Say what you really want to say, Viv. It's just me. You want to go out with him, right?"

"Yeah, but I don't want to deal with the bullshit," Vivian said.

"The Vivian I know doesn't generally give a damn what other folks think and will happily tell them so with a smile," I again reminded her of her own words.

"You're silly, Gigi. But you're right," Vivian said. "It's just a date. We're not getting married or anything. He seems like a cool brother, and I could use a night out with someone new."

"There you have it," I said. "I know your fast ass already said yes anyway, so when is your date?"

"Tomorrow at eight."

"I knew it!" I said, throwing my hands in the air.

∽ *Chapter Ten*

I hadn't seen Harper since the night we spent together after the contest a little over a month ago now. Because of all of my business travel, not only had I been missing stepping class, aside from my one private lesson from Cam, but I had also been unable to meet Harper when he invited me on a tea date a few weeks previously. I had been back in town for a few days when he sent me a text telling me he had an extra ticket to a Friday night steppers set. Turned out that we lived pretty close to one another, so we made plans to attend the set together.

When Harper and I arrived at the set, he introduced me to Lincoln Thomas, also known as Link, another stepper originally from Chicago. I had heard his name once before when Harper told me that the Minnesota contest winners, Rocco and Lena, were longtime students of his. Link had been dancing much longer than the twins and had developed his own, separate following in the Twin Cities. When we arrived, there were quite a few people I didn't recognize, even more than usual. I had been to a few sets by now and was beginning to at least recognize faces. Oh wait. There were Jada and Dawn, two of the top-tier members of the illustrious Secret Seven. No doubt there to spy on a non-twin-sponsored event. A little later on, the Furious Five arrived and took their usual place near the dance floor.

"Where are the regulars?" I asked Harper.

"You will probably see a few new faces here," Harper informed me with a smirk. "Given that the community is so small, I made the decision long ago that I would support any event that I chose."

"Why the division?" I wondered.

"Egos, personality conflicts, women, and of course the almighty dollar. You name it," Harper surmised. "Some of them are just plain old robots with no minds of their own. C'mon, let's dance!"

I was a little rusty since I had missed more than a few classes, but Harper always made me look as if I knew exactly what I was doing on the dance floor. It was good to be back out there.

We danced for two songs, and then Harper and I began to look for a seat. As he led me to an open seat at the bar, the parade of women we passed began to sound like a broken record: "Hey, Harp." "How you doin', Harper?" "Hey, cutie." I couldn't help but notice that for every tooth-filled female grin Harper received, I was on the receiving end of an equal number of glares, twisted lips, and eye rolling from those very same women. He offered a polite "hey" to each of them and didn't take any time at all to introduce me. As badly as I wanted to ask him, "What the hell is going on?" I thought it more prudent to get the story on the car ride home.

Since none of my safety nets from the twins' class were there for me to dance with, I sat at the bar for much of the night, checking out the scene and watching Harper make his way around the room. True to his gentlemanly form, he made sure to take the time to grab me every fourth or fifth song so that I didn't have to sit all night. During one of my stints at the bar, Link took a seat next to me.

"How's it going, Gigi? Glad to see that Harp is exposing you to something new."

"Well, everything is still pretty new to me right now. I have only been dancing for a few months," I replied.

"I was watching you out there," Link continued. "I see that you are a beginner to stepping, but let me ask, were you a dancer in your past life? Your foundation is pretty good for a beginner, and you seem to have no problem with catching the beat of the dance."

"Maybe I've just had great instructors so far."

Before he replied, Link gave me an expression that screamed disbelief. "Seriously, that may be, but some things cannot be taught."

"I danced ballet for over twelve years," I finally answered. "Not only does that seem like a lifetime ago, but it is very different from anything I am learning now."

"I knew it," Link confirmed. "It's not about *which* dance you learned, it's about grace and ability to feel the rhythm of the music you are dancing to. You know, I also teach stepping in the Twin Cities. My classes are across the river here in St. Paul, at the community center down the street. Here is my card. You should come and check us out sometime."

"C'mon, Ginger, last song of the night," Harper interrupted.

"Good to meet you, Gigi. Hope to see you back on this side of the river," Link said as I headed to the dance floor.

As the set ended, I felt prying eyes all over us as Harper helped me with my coat and took my hand as we headed for the door.

"Get ready for a few questions after tonight, Ginger," Harper warned on our drive home.

"What do you mean?"

"Well, number one, we showed up together. Number two, you were my first and my last dance of the night."

"So what if I was your first and last dance?"

"A man *always* has his first dance at a set with his girl. And then he makes a point to dance the last dance with her too. That tiny gesture lets other dancers know that the two are a couple."

"Oh. Are we a couple, Harper?"

I could hardly wait for the answer.

"People just talk, that's all. I'm sure there are no questions that you cannot handle," he said with a big grin.

Dang it. I wanted a better answer than that.

"I don't plan on doing anything but telling the truth," I replied.

Why not? I wondered.

"But speaking of questions, I certainly have a few," I said.

"Okay, what's up?"

"You're awfully popular with the female crowd, Mr. Drake. My goodness, even though I didn't know anyone at that set, they most certainly know you. I thought I was going to need sunglasses for all those big grins you were getting from women. Oh, and a shield for the stones some of them clearly wanted to throw at me."

"What are you talking about? I still haven't heard your question, Ginger," Harper said.

"Well, now I know why you don't bring this *girlfriend* of yours around too often—she must really cramp your style," I said, almost frowning.

"Oh you got jokes, huh?" Harper replied. "And stop frowning . . . you will put wrinkles on that beautiful face."

"Stop trying to distract me, Mr. Drake. Seriously, is there something I should know?" I asked.

"Ginger, I told you months ago that I have never been involved with any of these women who step, well, not involved enough to call them my girl."

Hmm. He's hedging.

"What I mean is I have socialized with a few steppers or met them for tea or a drink once or twice. Trust me when I say the looks you allegedly received tonight were more out of surprise than anything else. I always, *always* show up at a set alone, and I leave a set alone."

"Got it," I said. "So the smirks and snarls were because they thought I was your date for the evening."

"Well, you were, weren't you?"

At last, the answer I was waiting for.

∽

I read the name Cam as I answered my phone on the third ring.

"I heard you went to Link's set with Harper last night," Cam began his interrogation.

That dagnabbit Secret Seven, I thought. Instead of avoiding the cross-examination that was clearly about to occur, I dove in headfirst, spilled my guts voluntarily, and provided a debriefing to Cam.

"Personally, I don't have a problem with Link," Cam conceded. "There were some things that went down awhile back about soliciting students and sabotaging sets, but I don't get into the middle of all of that. How long did it take him to invite you to his classes?"

"Not long," I replied.

"Yeah, well, I think it is cool to check out as many classes as you want . . . as long as you know how to come home." I could hear Cam's smile over the phone. "In fact, Link's class is not the only other class around. There are a few other male instructors who started with CJ and me and decided to do their own thing. And for a while, there was a female instructor out of Chicago. This is where CJ and I disagree, again. Like I told you, he is completely territorial. If you start learning from him, you *must* stay with him, and you make sure that you scream it from the rooftops. I, on the other hand, think that we are grown folks who need to make our own decisions. If a person enjoys my class and my methods of teaching, they will always come back. When I hear that one of our regulars has attended another class, I genuinely want to know how the experience was and if there is something that CJ and I could do better."

"Hmm, seems like your brother takes loyalty to a whole

new level," I said.

"I always thought he might have taken a few too many hits to the head in his football days," Cam continued. "He has a good heart, and in fact wears it on his sleeve, but his disappointment can very easily be misperceived as intimidation. And you know that one thing grown folks, especially black grown folks, will not stand for is feeling like their ability to make their own decisions is somehow being compromised."

"Well, why don't you talk to him about that?" I asked.

Cam's loud laughter resonated through the phone line. "Were you not listening to me during our lesson a few weeks back? There is no point in trying to reason with that stubborn, headstrong brother of mine. He is unwavering when it comes to this dance."

"Too bad," I said.

"Yeah," Cam agreed. "Well, look, Gigi, I'm glad you enjoyed Link's set. I was just checking on you, but I see you are in good hands with Harp. Are you gonna make it to class next week?"

"Yep. No business travel, choir concerts, or conflicts of any kind for the next several weeks. Spring is here and summer is not far behind, so work will slow down a bit."

"Cool. See you there."

∞ *Chapter Eleven*

As I had promised Cam, I finally made it back to class the following week. Sasha and I had been keeping in touch over the phone, but it was really good to see her in class again. Although we hadn't known each other for too long, she confided in me and told me she had been dealing with some personal issues over the last few months. I gave her a big hug and we made a commitment to get together outside of class.

At the end of class, we stood in our usual circle introducing ourselves, meeting new students, and listening to announcements. Harper was already in the hallway near the exit, but I had a feeling he would wait for me to leave class. During announcements, CJ and Cam reminded us about their upcoming set to celebrate their birthdays on the fourth of July, which was just over a month away. They assured everyone that it would be the "set of all sets" with family and friends visiting from Chicago. They were selling tickets to the class at a discount if we purchased early, so Sasha and I bought our tickets and then spent a little time talking.

Sasha told me that things were tense between her and her husband, but she was still trying to stay positive and enjoy herself when she could.

"Is it the dancing that is causing trouble?" I asked.

"No," she answered. "I asked him if he thought I was

spending too much time away from home, and he told me he was happy that I had a new interest."

"Well, I know we don't know each other that well, honey, but you can always share with me. I guarantee that I will just be an ear for you," I assured her.

"I appreciate that, Gigi," Sasha said with a small smile. "Some of our friends that have known us as a couple for years say it's the seven-year itch and we'll get through it. I am starting to think that Negro may be scratching."

"Like I said, anytime. You want to get together for a drink this week?" I offered.

"Sure, that sounds good. I will give you a call."

I gave Sasha another hug, and soon I was headed for the door.

Harper was still standing in the hallway by the door. He extended his arm and walked me to my car. No sooner than I could ask him what was on his mind did he casually inform me that his "tenacious girlfriend" would be joining him for the twins' birthday set.

"She is close friends with a group of women who follow Cam's music career, so they come to his birthday party every year," Harper began to explain. "I didn't want to show up with her out of the blue without telling you."

"Well, that would have been okay, Harper," I convincingly lied. "Unless that means you can't save me a dance, why would I have a problem with it?"

"We have been spending time together. I just thought I should let you know. And of course I am going to dance with you! You are my prized pupil," he whispered.

Naturally I wasn't excited to hear about Harper's plans for the twins' birthday set, but we were just becoming friends and he had been honest with me up front. I admit that I was curious about this so-called girlfriend. I soon rationalized that it would be good to see how he interacted with her in a public setting.

"We still have more than a month until that set—want to grab some tea and do a little dancing sometime this weekend?" Harper asked.

"Sure," I answered. "Let me see what my girls have planned for me this weekend, but I bet I can get away for a few hours."

"Or I could come to you," Harper suggested. "I mean, do you have hardwood floors in your kitchen or anywhere else in your home? We don't need that much space to practice."

Wow. I hadn't thought about bringing this dance into my home. Or more importantly, bringing in a man to meet my daughters. I had made enough bad decisions in that area of my life.

"I will give you a call and let you know, dear," I said with a smile.

"Groovy," Harper said.

⁂

"Hey, you two, how do you feel about Mom practicing her dancing here in the kitchen?" I asked Grace and Isabel as we were having dinner that night.

"It's not like we don't see you doing that silly stepping all the time, Mom," answered Grace.

"No, I mean if I bring one of my . . . instructors here to help me practice," I clarified.

"I don't care," Grace replied.

"I don't care either," Isabel chimed in. "Which one of your teachers would come?"

"His name is Harper Drake. He is not one of the lead instructors, but he helps out in class and I like dancing with him. He's good at teaching me the things I need to learn to get better."

They both stopped eating and looked at each other, then looked at me.

"Why are you smiling so much, Mom? Do you like this Harper dude?" Grace asked.

I am still wondering why this is her given name since it is her absolute worst quality.

"Yes, I like him. He's very nice. You guys can meet him for yourselves if you're okay with him stopping by."

"You mean we have to watch?" Grace asked.

I smirked. "No, I won't tie you to a chair or anything, but it wouldn't kill you to see how I have been spending my time lately when I'm not here."

"I think I will make a video," Isabel added.

"I don't think I am ready for movies, Isabel."

"Sure, Mom, bring this teacher of yours so we can check him out," Grace concluded.

"Shut up, Grace!" Isabel started. "Mom said she likes dancing with him and he's a good teacher. So I want to see them dance!"

"You shut up, Isabel!" Grace retaliated. "I can check out anybody that comes into our house if I want to. And besides, I can tell you like him, Mom. Your smile is way too big."

"Both of you be quiet and finish your dinner."

I ended the conversation, no doubt with a giant smile.

∽

A few weeks later, the kids were out of school for the summer. It was a good time to invite Harper to the house for tea and a private lesson.

"Very nice to meet you ladies." Harper extended his hand after I introduced him to Grace and Isabel.

"So, what exactly do you do, Harper—just dance?" Grace remarked.

"No, ma'am, I sell real estate," Harper answered.

"Oh." Grace smiled wryly. "Mom is the best decorator in town."

"I am beginning to find that out for myself," Harper nodded.

As usual, Isabel had been quiet and listening to the conversation.

"Let's pop in some music!" Harper said as he spun around on one foot.

Isabel giggled and set her iPad to record.

The girls were in and out of the room while Harper and I danced over the next hour. I told him what I had worked on during my lesson with Cam so he helped me work on smoothing out those turns, and he also gave me variations of signals for the extended right turn and the roll-out-roll-back. It was always fun dancing with Harper. We laughed a lot, but I also learned a lot. I remembered one of the first things Stacey told me about him was his level of patience for new dancers. She had certainly been right about that.

"Nice work, Ginger." Harper applauded me at the end of our hour.

"That wasn't too terrible," Grace said, "but why are you calling Mom by her middle name?"

"Don't you like your mom's middle name?" Harper asked.

"It's okay, but you still didn't answer my question," Grace persisted.

"Mom, I have your dance on video!" Isabel interrupted.

"Yes, and I will need that video to add to my collection," Harper teased. I think.

Harper and I headed toward the front door, closely followed by the girls.

"It was very nice to meet you, Grace and Isabel. I hope to see you again," Harper said.

"Nice to meet you too," Isabel said.

"You and Mom are pretty silly together, but you seem okay so I guess you can come back," Grace remarked. "It was nice to meet you too, Harper."

"Thanks, I think," Harper said with a smirk. "And, by the way, I call your mom 'Ginger' because I think it is the most beautiful of her three names."

"Um . . . okay," Grace said as she shrugged her shoulders.

"I'll walk you out," I said as Harper changed his shoes at

the door. After tying his laces, Harper took my hand and we walked out to my driveway.

"They're a tough crowd, but they love their mom," I said as we stood at Harper's car door.

"They're not so tough. They are protective of you for good reason, as they should be," Harper added. "Good class today. You are coming along nicely."

"Thanks," I said as I clapped my hands.

"See you soon, Ginger."

Harper kissed me on the cheek and I headed back into the house to get Harper's report card from the girls.

"He seemed nice, Mom," Isabel concluded.

"Anybody who makes you smile for a whole hour must be okay, *Ginger*," Grace added.

"Cut it out, Gracie. And yes, Isabel, he's a very nice guy," I said as I began to make dinner.

∽ *Chapter Twelve*

Harper and I were able to fit in one more lesson, and then July was upon us before we knew it. Sasha and I were totally excited about the twins' birthday set. I couldn't wait to hear Cam on that trumpet! Besides that, Sasha and I had been dancing now for almost eight months and felt like we could finally hold our own on the dance floor . . . within reason. It had been an excruciatingly hot Fourth of July weekend, so I was sure I was about to be amazed by some ridiculously scantily clad female steppers. Seems like the phrase "just because you can get your body into it doesn't mean you should wear it" meant absolutely nothing to this crowd. But I digress.

The set was being held at a local night club where Cam was known to perform on occasion. The brothers had rented out the entire place for their birthday party. It was nicely decorated and had an outdoor patio area to escape the inevitable heat that would build up inside. I noticed there were quite a few men I didn't recognize, but then I remembered the twins telling us in class that folks would be in town from their Chicago neighborhood to help them celebrate. Sasha and I were at the bar collecting our customary glasses of wine when Harper stepped in with a woman on his arm.

I admit that I was caught a little off guard, but I was glad now that he had told me. Harper and I had had more than a few great lessons and we had shared some pretty wonderful moments over the last few months; I suppose it's no wonder that I had almost forgotten that *she* was coming. Sasha pulled me away from the bar and out onto the patio.

"Are you okay?" Sasha asked.

"Of course," I answered. "Harper and I are just friends, and besides that, he told me he was bringing someone. Apparently his girl follows Cam's music career, so she always comes to his birthday party."

"Okay, I know you two have been hanging out, so just making sure," Sasha continued. "But if you really are okay, maybe you could try a little harder to untwist your lip on that side of your mouth."

We both started laughing.

"C'mon, girl," I said as I snapped back to reality. "Let's go show all these men what we can do on that dance floor."

We headed back inside with liquid courage in our hands.

A few minutes later, CJ and Cam were thanking everyone for coming to their party and giving orders to eat, drink, and dance. Before I knew it, I was being pulled onto the dance floor by a visitor from Chicago.

The room was so steamy that I was already beginning to sweat only a few minutes into the dance. This gentleman was very smooth on the dance floor and even better at holding my waist tightly. He was respectful and gentle, though, reminiscent of a dance with Cam.

He walked me back to my seat after two songs. I could hardly wait to pull out that fan.

Cam had taken the stage and was beginning to play.

Others were still on the dance floor, but I couldn't take my eyes off of him. He was so wonderful on that instrument. Smooth and melodious just like his dance. I hoped I wasn't salivating. Just as I began to check the corners of my mouth for drool, Harper sat down next to me.

"He's something on that horn, isn't he?" Harper asked.

"Hey you," I replied. "Yes, he is pretty incredible all right."

"You missed a spot," Harper said, pretending to wipe dribble from the corner of my mouth with my napkin.

"Be quiet," I said, blushing a little. "I saw you come in. So, where is she?"

"*She* is at the stage clamoring at Cam like a groupie." Harper smirked.

"Oh" was all I could say.

"May I have this dance?" It was Link who was reaching for my hand.

"Catch you later, Harper," I said as I took Link's hand and headed to the dance floor.

I hadn't seen Link since his set in St. Paul almost three months ago. I recalled that I was still super new to the dance at that time, so this would be my first dance with Mr. Lincoln Thomas.

It was nice. He was very gracious, but he must have taken my ballet comment to heart because I was turning on that dance floor like I had never turned before. Nothing scary, just totally showy. Link was definitely a bit of a hot dog. He gave me subtle cues about what was coming next so that our dance appeared flawless . . . almost. He tried a double left spin once, and trust me when I say the resulting dip was an artistic disguise for what would have otherwise been a tragically embarrassing crash onto the floor by yours truly. He was good at cleaning it up. I guess that's what happens after being a stepper for over thirty years.

The song ended and Link gave me a hug. On the way back to my chair, I noticed that Harper was on the dance floor with Sasha. I didn't even make it back to my seat before another Chi-town visitor took me by the hand.

And that was pretty indicative of how the evening went. Dance after dance after dance after dance. I felt like the belle of the ball. Sasha and I were having a great time and barely had the chance to finish our first glass of wine.

After about half an hour, I had finally made it back to my seat in search of a glass of water. I sat for a minute, absorbing the vibe of the room. The DJ was lighting up the place with hot tracks between Cam's trumpet performances. The fellowship, the laughter, the good food, the dance. So many great dancers. And then there was *Michael the Great.* Cam was right. No matter how crowded the dance floor, and tonight it was particularly packed, Michael always danced as if he and his current victim were the only two on the floor. Bumping into other couples and completely ignoring lane control for his partner. I had been lucky enough to dodge him and his dance for the last eight months because he was one of those who thought he was too good to dance with a beginner. I was totally fine with that and hoped he would view me as a beginner forever. Aside from the look of terror on Michael's partner, everyone on that dance floor was having a wonderful time. Turning and spinning, gliding and flowing. I was taking it all in.

Cam was back onstage, ready to amaze us once again with the melodies of his trumpet, and I was ready to listen. Suddenly there was a loud noise and the music stopped almost instantly. I stood from my chair to look toward the disruption coming from the other side of the room near the patio.

CJ and Link were facing one another with angry glares. All the while, their respective followers were gathering behind them on opposing sides. I started to think about the rumble scene from *West Side Story*. Any minute now I was expecting the Jets and the Sharks to appear on the scene and battle it out in graceful leaps and rhythmic snapping. I suppose this would be a stepping rumble instead to see who could do the best footwork.

I couldn't hear everything that was being said, but it was clearly a disagreement of epic proportions. I was just barely able to make out a few setences that sounded something like this:

"I've been dancing twice as long as you have! Why do you think you know more than me? You ain't shit!"

And:

"The fact that you've been dancing thirty years just means your ass is old. It doesn't mean you know everything!"

Several steppers were packing up their belongings and beginning to leave. Sasha sat next to me, and we both wondered if we should be doing the same.

Cam left his post onstage and calmly but quickly walked

over to where the two were about to "throw down," if that's what men who are almost fifty call it. I still could barely make out what was being said, but the body language spoke volumes. At one point, CJ and Link were just inches apart from one other, screaming in each others' faces. As the exchange of profanity was reaching new heights, I saw Cam step between the two of them and place his right hand on CJ's chest as if to say, "Chill out, bro." Then CJ quickly gave the order for his crew to stand down. Almost immediately, Link did the same. John, the twins' number-one knight, helped to disperse the angry miniature mob. Link shook Cam's hand and headed toward his car in the parking lot.

"Sorry about the disturbance, folks," Cam said, trying to refocus the party. "Men turn forty-nine, and what's left of our hormones start raging out of control!"

A few of us chuckled lightly, but understandably so, the tension remained high.

"Let me play something to soothe the savage beast that is my brother," Cam continued.

There was a crowd of women gathered around CJ, making sure that he was intact. Naturally, the Secret Seven were included in the concerned entourage. As Cam played an inspired slow tune on his trumpet, several of the remaining couples took the floor to dance. But they weren't doing the typical "slow grind" I was accustomed to seeing on the dance floor. I wasn't sure, but I thought it must have been another form of stepping.

"It's called *walking*," Stacey whispered in my ear. "It's a form of slow dancing, but not quite the 'slow grind' we grew up doing and watching."

"You're right. It doesn't look like slow dancing at all, at least for some of these pairs. They literally look like they are just *walking* around the floor," I said.

"Right," Stacey continued. "Similar to stepping, you still move with your partner around the perimeter of the floor, but instead of turns and spins, you *walk* or take steps to the slow beat of the music. It can be a close, romantic dance, or it can also be more casual. Steppers use walking as an alternative to traditional close-in slow dancing so that they are able to dance with more than one partner and maintain both the respect for the woman and the integrity of the dance. There is no particular count to walking either. You move your body in sync with your partner to the groove of the music. I think that's what makes it so sensual . . . with the right partner."

"Cool," I said.

At that moment, Stacey walked toward CJ, as his entourage had cleared a bit. She gave him a hug and pulled him out onto the dance floor. Stacey and CJ began to dance. I could tell this wasn't a first for those two. He seemed to have calmed down now, but Stacey always had a way of neutralizing an otherwise tense situation. Despite the crazy confrontation that had just occurred, I think we were all beginning to remember that we were celebrating at a birthday party.

During the next hour or so, the birthday cake was cut and the line dancers had their opportunity to hit the floor. I noticed that Eleana was trying to pick up a few steps on the fly while Ivy was giving her on-the-floor training as the dance moved along.

It was close to midnight now and I was ready to leave. My feet were exhausted and I was perspiring from head to toe. Sasha and I grabbed our bags and stood to leave when I realized I didn't get my dance with Harper. I quickly searched the room for him to at least wave good-bye, but I wasn't able to spot him. I decided I would give him a call tomorrow.

As we left the set, we wished another happy birthday to both Cam and CJ and gave each of them big hugs near the exit.

"Sorry again about that mess," CJ apologized. "Hope you still had a good time."

"Of course," I assured him. "We had a ball! My feet will be sore for days to prove it!"

CJ smiled as Sasha and I headed for the door.

∽ *Chapter Thirteen*

The more people I met as I continued to step, the more friends I made on Facebook. It was amazing what you could learn about folks through social media these days. Relationship statuses went from married to single overnight. God-fearing Christians praised the Lord one minute and talked trash about folks the next. Of course, Facebook was great for seeing pictures, connecting with friends and family, and even keeping current with community events and birthdays. But it never failed that the day following a steppers' set, Facebook pages were on fire. And the twins' birthday set was certainly no exception. In fact, my Facebook timeline had never seen so much activity.

Apparently the "CJ/Link face-off," as it had been dubbed in less than twenty-four hours, was not the only talk of the night. In fact, it had quickly taken a backseat to a woman scorned and accusing an unnamed "she-stepper" of being a home wrecker and making inappropriate public advances toward her husband. I had also obviously missed a confrontation between line dancers who had been arguing across pages of posts about two different versions of a line dance and which one was the true "original."

At this point, I think it bears repeating that these steppers made up a "mature" crowd. Never mind the tact, these Negroes were old.

"Mom, some of these posts look like the stuff that goes around at school," Grace said, reading my Facebook page over my shoulder.

"Well, Gracie, when you bring men and women together in a social setting, regardless of age, there is going to be conflict."

I did read one post that morning that made me pause. It wasn't lengthy or spouting anything derogatory or remotely inappropriate. It was simple and straightforward and made me wonder for the first time about my future in this dance:

"Steppin' used to be fun. Times have changed."

After glancing through a few more posts, I decided to give Cam a call to see if I could get any answers as to why such a spectacle would occur between two perfectly grown up and otherwise respectable men.

"There is some personal history between those two, but what it really comes down to is jealousy. That's the only explanation," Cam reasoned.

"What?" I questioned.

"You see, G, this dance is not just about the dance. It is about who can do it the biggest and best. When division and separation sets in and some of us do it bigger and better than others, the egos, jealousy, and of course the money takes on a life of its own," Cam continued. "We are men after all."

And there you have it: testosterone at its finest.

"That's it?" I asked. "But who is jealous of whom? Men can't put aside their personal feelings for the good of business? That doesn't make any sense to me, especially when all of you can be, and already are, equally successful. It seems to me that Link and you two have a great and separate following in the Twin Cities."

"Spoken like a true woman," Cam concluded. "Please understand that is a compliment. No disrespect intended. Men let their egos turn them into idiots. Women can be— well, I will just say it—*evil* at times, but at the end of the day, they can put that aside and handle business."

"Well, that is very big of you to admit," I acknowledged.

"I had a wonderful mother," Cam explained. "I watched it happen before my own eyes. She supported my father's music dreams even when we couldn't afford it. And she always made sure that the business of the home was handled. You must know what that's like as a single mom, Gigi."

"Boy do I," I agreed.

"But back to the incident from the other night," Cam continued. "I must personally apologize for things getting out of hand. We always try our best to promote a mature environment, but we failed miserably. Hope it didn't ruin your good time."

"Of course not," I said. "I had a really great time and got my feet wet dancing with a lot of different steppers. Thanks, but no need for the apology. It was fun."

"Good," Cam said. "That's what's up."

∽

Are you busy? My phone beeped with a text message from Harper a few hours later.

No, I replied. My phone rang a few seconds after I hit send.

"You know you can call and see if I pick up instead of texting first," I said with a little sarcasm.

"I guess that's right," Harper admitted. "Just didn't want to disturb you if you were busy."

"What's going on?" I asked. "I was gonna call you today, so good timing, Mr. Drake."

"Not much going on. Did you enjoy the set last night?"

"It was a really good time. The twins looked so handsome. And Cam on that trumpet! Wow!" I exclaimed. "But what about that crazy standoff?"

"Yeah, I know. Crazy brothers. Try to promote an adult, drama-free atmosphere and then stuff like that pops off," Harper opined. "They could have taken that bullshit behind closed doors."

"Well, it certainly added to the entertainment," I commented, "and it was still a great time."

"I noticed you didn't do much sitting," Harper continued. "I told you your dance card would be full."

"Well," I said, realizing Harper's tone had changed, "what did you think of the set? Did your girl have a good time?"

"I don't know. She spent most of the time talking to her girlfriends and drinking. We danced a few times. Every time I tried to grab you up for a dance, you were already on the floor."

"It's not as though you were sitting alone in a corner all night, Harper. You were all over that dance floor all night long as usual," I reminded him.

"I know, I know," he admitted.

"What is this really about, Harper?" I prodded.

Silence.

"Harper, are you okay?"

"Yes. Look, I'm gonna be straight with you, Ginger. Watching you smile and look so damn happy dancing with all those other steppers, man, I just wasn't feeling it."

What the fuck? Was he for real? Just like a man. He brought his *girlfriend* to a party and then tried to control what I was doing? Really?

Before I had a chance to really light into him and let him have it, he continued.

"Don't get me wrong—I am so glad that you are learning to love the dance. But every time I saw you dancing with someone else, I don't know. I wanted to be the one making you smile on the dance floor."

"Oh." He was becoming an expert at placing me at a loss for words.

"I know I sound like a selfish asshole for saying something like that," Harper acknowledged.

"Yep," I said with a laugh, "but it's kinda sweet too. Let me guess . . . did you fail *sharing* in kindergarten?"

"Hell yeah! Nobody was allowed to touch my Tinker-toys," Harper joked.

I was starting to realize that Harper was a pretty funny guy, in a quirky, cynical kind of way.

"Seriously, Ginger," Harper went on, "you're cool and I enjoy your company. Would you be okay if we spent more time together?"

"Absolutely, Mr. Drake."

∽ *Chapter Fourteen*

Over the next few weeks, Harper and I went to see a movie and had a few more private lessons. I was still going to class, but it soon became pretty obvious to the others that Harper and I had been dancing together outside of class.

Each week, both during and after class, Harper would make his way over to me and we would have our own "private" dance apart from the rest of the class. We generally waited until it was open dance time so that everyone else was also dancing, but my routine of leaving right after class was noticeably different. My face hurt from smiling so much during those dances after class. Now and again, Harper would sneak a kiss on my cheek or whisper something in my ear to make my face hurt even more.

This particular week, Harper had to leave class early, so he was unable to walk me to my car. Instead, Vivian was my escort to the parking lot.

"Um, Gigi," Vivian started, "what the hell is going on between you and Harper?"

"What do you mean?" I asked.

"Don't bullshit me, G," she continued. "Everybody can see y'all are all goo-goo eyed during class and then again during open dance. Those dances after class seem a little steamy to me! You taking privates?"

"Harper and I have danced a few times outside of class when I've had to travel, Vivian," I answered. "That's all!"

"I thought you were taking privates from Cam?" Vivian inquired.

"I had one with Cam, and he knows that I dance with Harper too. In fact, Cam encouraged me to continue dancing with Harper. He said that he could tell that my dance was improving."

"Hmm . . . if you say so. But the way you two are grinning at each other—"

"Shut up, Viv!" I interrupted. "Anyway, what's been happening with you and Mr. DJ?"

"Girl, I don't know. I am pretty sure that he is seeing other women. I don't care because I am still talking to other dudes, but I think he lies to me about it."

"Does it bug you? Tell him!" I advised.

"I just don't understand it since we never said we'd be exclusive or anything. He's something to do for now, so I'm gonna leave it alone."

"Only if you're okay with it, Viv," I said.

"Now quit trying to change the subject. You and Harper?" Vivian pried again.

"Look, Viv, we dance together. We drink tea. Our businesses intersect. So, yes, we hang out on occasion. And, yes, I like him," I finally admitted.

"Ooh!" Vivian howled in a schoolgirl tone.

"You are silly," I said.

"You two are kinda cute together, G. But this steppin' thing . . . like I always tell you: be careful. These dudes are a stone cold trip. Trip!" Vivian exclaimed. "That reminds me. The twins are taking a group of us on a road trip to Milwaukee in a few months. Ivy is having a line dance party, and both Stacey and I are going. It should be fun, and we can get a chance to dance with the Mil-town men. I like dancing with that crowd."

"I don't know, Viv. Traveling with this dance?" I asked. "I already travel so much for work, but I'll think about it."

"Okay," Vivian answered. "So, when are you two love-birds getting back together?"

Vivian made a kissing motion with her lips.

"We have a tea date next week," I said with a big smile.

"Have fun, and be careful, girl," Vivian repeated, "Oh! And start thinking about that trip!"

⤴

The following week after class, Harper and I sat in our favorite spot at his favorite tea bar, talking about the trios we had been working on earlier that evening. Dancing as a threesome was new to me, so Harper was giving me a few pointers when I realized it was getting late and I should be heading home.

"That reminds me. Why didn't we have our usual private dance after class tonight?" I asked Harper on our way to the car.

"I've been meaning to talk to you about that," Harper answered as he reached for my hand.

"What's up?"

"I got a call from CJ last week when he heard about our private lessons. I told you he could be a bit territorial, so I think we should take a break for awhile. You took a private from Cam a while back. Maybe you should reach back out to him if you can't make it to class."

"Oh really," I said as I dropped Harper's hand, instantly and completely irritated by his words. "Well, you will recall that the only reason I took *one* private lesson from Cam was because *you* needed a break after the contest."

Arms crossed, I continued. "How about this: when you decide that you are allowed to give me lessons again, give me a call, Harper. Or do they get to tell you who you are allowed to talk to on a personal level, as well?"

"C'mon, Ginger, don't take it like that. It's not my class! I don't need the brothers thinking I am trying to steal their students."

"It shouldn't matter, Harper," I said as I threw my hands in the air. "Cam told me as long as I was learning the dance and having a good time, it didn't matter who I took lessons from. Come to think of it, you said CJ contacted you, not Cam, right?"

"That's right," Harper said.

"Cool. While you boys are measuring your dicks, I think I will just take Link up on his offer and start attending his classes for a while."

"Over the top, Ms. Grant. Over the top."

"See you later, Harper," I said as I got into my car.

Now I was frustrated. And when a girl is frustrated, she takes action. I found Link's card in the bottom of my bag and called him before I even made it home. He was more than happy to hear that I would be in attendance at his next class.

∽

A few hours later, I found myself sipping a glass of wine at Stacey's home.

"Stacey, I am going to Link's class next week," I said.

"What happened, Gigi?"

"I have just decided to try something new."

"Uh, you have been stepping for all of eight months. What do you mean *new*?" Stacey asked.

"Okay, look, I am already finding out that as old as all these steppers are, this mess is all too silly. I took one lesson from Cam, who apparently told CJ I had a few privates from Harper, and now CJ is telling Harper——"

"Oh boy. Already? CJ can be territorial, but——"

"Territorial!" I shrieked. "I've been in that class for eight months and now I suddenly owe them some loyalty?"

"Relax, honey," Stacey said. "You already know there is something crazy between CJ and Link. You sure you want to get in the middle of that? Besides, CJ is overreacting. I'm sure he doesn't really think you're doing anything wrong by taking lessons from Harper."

"Well, he pissed me off," I added. "Harper, too, for that matter. If he's gonna punk out every time CJ says something to him, then——"

"Again, relax. Look at it from Harper's point of view for a

second. He has a point. If you are paying him for lessons and you are a student in the twins' class, then that's money that one of them could potentially be making. Remember, this is business, honey. On the other hand, I know you and Harper have a personal thing going on, so I see why it's bothering you too."

I nodded.

"Gigi, you told me yourself that Cam said it's good to take other classes. Link certainly produces winning dancers, so give it a shot. You going alone?"

"Yeah, the first time anyway," I answered. "I will see how it goes after that."

"Okay. Give it a try and see how you like it. Maybe you'll be able to show me a few things after a lesson or two with Link."

Stacey smiled as she gave me a hug.

As I drove home, I wondered if Stacey was right. Maybe I was overreacting to Harper's decision. The problem was that I could feel myself really starting to like him, so, right or wrong, that automatically pushed my defense mechanisms into high alert. Maybe a break from my class routine would be good for me. And maybe a little break would be good for me and Harper. And who knows, maybe it would be good for my dance, too.

∞ *Chapter Fifteen*

Over the next three weeks, I attended Link's class, distancing myself from the twins' class. And from Harper. We exchanged a few "pleasant" text messages, but that was about it.

Link's class was conducted in a totally different manner than the twins'. For starters, there were noticeably more men. It was also much smaller. Never more than about seven women and an equal number of men. Because the number was equal, we spent most of the time working on combinations during class. I was Link's newest student, so he often chose me as his partner for much of the class.

I met Lena and Rocco, the Minnesota winning couple from the twins' contest a few months ago. They were a very nice pair and had been dancing together for as long as they had been married, almost five years. They told me that they began learning the eight count when they asked the twins to teach them how to step for their first dance as man and wife. After the wedding, they decided to give Link a try and never looked back.

I couldn't believe the level of separation within the steppers' community in such a small place as the Twin Cities. There weren't that many of us to start with, but who was I to question anything? I was only a nine-month-old stepper, but I had already gotten a taste of the madness.

"Today's combination is going to focus on connecting turns," Link started. "We will do an extended right into a reverse and end with a roll-out-roll-back. Fellas, I need you to change positions from the weak to the strong side of the ladies and be sure to give various signals."

Link demonstrated the move twice with Lena. It was beautiful.

"C'mon, Gigi. I know this is advanced for you, but I got you."

And he was right. After about three attempts, I was catching all of Link's signals.

"See, I told you," Link said with a big smile. "It's just about having confidence in your dance and trusting that your partner is not leading you astray."

We worked on variations of that combination for the next forty-five minutes, and then it was time to go. Link asked me to stay after class for a minute to talk.

"Thanks for waiting, Gigi," Link said.

"Sure," I replied. "What's going on?"

"It's no secret that I've enjoyed having you in my class these past few weeks. You really have a great basic foundation of the dance. I'm actually surprised that you're a student coming out of the twins' class," Link snidely remarked.

"Oh no. I'm not getting into any of that," I said, putting my hands over my ears.

Link laughed. "Seriously, though, you are a great follower."

I figured that there was no reason to tell him that Harper got much of the credit for my skill level so far.

"Thanks," I said.

"I know this is probably the furthest thing from your mind right now, but have you ever considered competing in a beginners' contest?"

"What?" I exclaimed.

"Told you this would take you by surprise," Link said with a grin. "In about three months, there is a beginner/ instructor contest in Chicago. I would like you to consider being my partner."

"Three months. Are you kidding?" I thought I was hearing things.

"Not at all," Link continued. "You have it in you, Gigi. If we work at it together, I know that you would be ready. Look, this is the first time you are hearing about it, so don't say no just yet. Promise me you will think about it."

"Promise," I said.

"Okay. See you next week?" Link asked.

"I'll be here," I answered.

∽

On the way home from Link's class, I was still a little dazed from the conversation that had just happened. I began to imagine the fallout from the twins when Link began calling me *his* student after only a few weeks of practice. I began to imagine competing in front of a crowd. I began to imagine that Link's intentions were perhaps not as pure as he tried to make them out to be.

I was doing such a great job of freaking myself out that I didn't even notice I had a missed call until I pulled into my garage. It was Harper. He had left me a voice mail message:

"Hey, Ginger, it's Harper Drake. I know you're still mad at me, but get over it. It's been a few weeks and I want to talk to you about something. Hit me up when you get a chance."

I played the message four times because I missed hearing his voice. I was still pretty angry about something as silly as a five-dollar class, but it had been almost three weeks since I had seen Harper, so I had to call him back.

"Hey," I said when he answered the phone.

"Hey yourself," Harper replied. "Look, I apologize again for the misunderstanding. I know you think that the twins can tell me what to do and who to teach, but I've been doing this for a while. One of the ways I have been able to stay neutral is by not overstepping into any person's business affairs. And believe me, G, this is a business, the *only* business for a lot of these cats. But that is no excuse for me to cut you off under any circumstances."

"Okay," I said.

"So, the reason I wanted to talk was to invite you on a quick road trip."

I was grinning now ear to ear.

"CJ and Cam are pulling a group of Untouchable Steppers together for a road trip to Milwaukee. It's the fifth anniversary for one of the steppers' organizations in town, and CJ asked me to come and help him out with a few workshops over the weekend."

Still grinning, but a little less now.

"I know you are tight with Vivian and Stacey, but I was taking a chance that you hadn't made plans to go yet."

"Yep, both Viv and Stacey asked me if I was interested in going with them. It sounds like fun, but they are spending almost four days there, and I can't get that kind of time away from work or the kids right now."

"I am going Friday night coming home Sunday morning," Harper said.

"Are you asking me to ride shotgun, Harper?"

"Yes, ma'am, affirmative. I admit I miss hanging out with you, and I thought we could catch up on everything on the ride."

"Hmm. So we show up together at a set *out of town*. You aren't concerned about the misperception or the allegations of pilfering students? I don't want you to tarnish your Swiss neutrality."

"You are such a wise ass, Ginger," Harper said, chuckling. "Trust me when I say that money and class will be the absolute furthest thing from anyone's mind when we show up together. Folks will get the message."

"And what message is that?" I asked.

"That Harper can get down however he wants to get down!"

"You said that with some authority," I remarked, "and in the third person."

"Hell yeah," Harper continued. "Besides, you will be the one who gets all the questions, not me."

"Way to stand up for a girl," I said.

"You know I got you," he assured me. "Those steppers can think whatever they want. Anyway, we haven't danced in quite a while now. Can't wait to see what Link has *tried* to teach you over the past few weeks."

I could tell he was trying to change the subject and avoid more of my questions, so I let him, for now.

"Oh you get ready," I said. "I just might surprise you on that dance floor. Link thinks I'm a natural."

"I just bet he does."

∽ Chapter Sixteen

It was the morning of our road trip to Milwaukee, and the weather was perfect for a drive. The leaves were just barely on the brink of changing to autumn colors, the skies were clear and bright, and the air was crisp.

I had given both Stacey and Vivian the heads-up that I was going to be coming with Harper. Naturally, Vivian thought it was hilarious and said she couldn't wait to have her camera ready for all the chins that were sure to hit the floor. Her DJ wasn't going to be around, so I was sure she would be there to instigate. Stacey was supportive. She agreed not to tell CJ or Cam ahead of time, especially when I hadn't been to their classes for over a month since that craziness about who should take a private lesson from whom.

"The brothers will be happy to have you back, even if you have decided to take privates from Harper," Stacey reasoned.

"Well, that will be cool, but I want to see how things go first. I'm not happy about the madness over a simple class, and I really do like the twins, but I'm not getting in the middle of any mess."

"Um, I hear you, but what exactly do you think you are creating by showing up with Harper, Gigi?"

"I like Harper. He's funny, we get along, and he's a great

dancer. He already told me people are going to talk, and if he's cool with it, so am I. Besides, this is about the dance, right?"

"Uh-huh," answered Stacey. "See you in Mil-town, G. Tell Harp hi, and you two be safe on the road. Just curious— are you two staying in a room together?"

Oh shoot. I hadn't even thought about it.

"As soon as I know, I will let you know," I said, wondering myself what the answer would be. "I will text you as soon as we make it to town, Stace."

∞

"So how does your *girlfriend* feel about you taking a road trip with another chick, Mr. Drake?" I asked Harper about fifteen minutes into our drive to Milwaukee.

"She just came back from a cruise with some dude," Harper said, sounding annoyed. "I don't think I need her permission for a stepping road trip with you."

Silence for a minute. I didn't know if I should say anything more or not. He was clearly annoyed, but was he angry?

"Don't get me wrong, Ginger. Like I told you, we see other people. And whatever you do, don't think I asked you to come with me just because she decided to do what she did."

He was reading my mind.

"Hell, if someone offered to take me on a Caribbean cruise, I might go too!" Harper laughed, but only for a second. "It's her typical M.O.—she wants me to compete for her attention and I am just not the one. Hmm. Or maybe *she's* not the one."

"Okay," I said, "you will tell me more about that—or not—when you're ready."

"Nothing more to tell. I am where I want to be and with whom I want to be with. Let's focus on the weekend and have fun on that dance floor. That reminds me, are you planning to come to the workshops?"

"Um, I haven't paid for them in advance. I will probably check out one or the other. Which one are you teaching?"

"I am helping CJ in tomorrow's workshop. I'm not sure we will get there in time for the one tonight."

"I know the girls are wanting to hang out once I make it to town. Even though I haven't learned any line dances yet, Ivy is hosting a line dance wine and dine for the ladies. I thought that sounded like fun."

"Of course. I have no doubt that you ladies will have plenty to talk about. I'm sure the brothers will hit me up so we can all be on the same page for the workshop tomorrow. We will get settled in and see each other when we see each other. I'm just glad you agreed to come with me."

"I'm glad you invited me," I said as I playfully rubbed the top of his head. "But speaking of 'settled in,' I can't believe I didn't think to reserve a room for myself."

"I invited you, so I figured I would take care of that. I hope you don't mind that I reserved a two-bedroom suite. It was a little more cost efficient than two separate rooms. There is only one bathroom, but the bedrooms have separate doors and everything. I know how you ladies are with your bathrooms, so I can use the one in the hall if I need to."

There was that sense of humor again.

"Don't be ridiculous, Harper," I said. "I should be able to spare you a solid five or ten minutes in the bathroom."

He glared at me and I smiled back.

"Anyway, it will be fine," he said. "I know the last time we spent the night together, we stayed up until daybreak talking, so I will try not to keep you up all night running my mouth."

"The way I remember it, we were both running our mouths . . . and practicing a dip!"

"Right, right. Hope you remember that dip, because you're gonna get it this weekend," Harper promised.

"Oh, I am more than ready, Mr. Drake."

∽

Harper and I had almost six hours to fill. We talked about the weather. We talked about families. We talked about places we had visited and would like to visit. Turned out we both loved to travel. And, of course, we talked about stepping. Harper told me that I would notice some immediate differences on the dance floor in Milwaukee. He told me that the style of dance was different than Chicago and what we were learning in the Twin Cities. The dance was less regimented and the women had a different flow. He said I would know what he meant once I saw it.

"One more thing you should know. The dudes can be a little . . . hands on. I don't think they will be inappropriate, but some of their moves are a little more suggestive than what you are accustomed to, so I want you to be aware. That's another reason I wanted you to come to the workshop. It will be good to dance with a few of them before the set tomorrow night."

"Thanks for the heads-up," I replied. "So, how does this workshop play out? Do you and the twins teach in conjunction with a Milwaukee group, or are you guest instructors for the day?"

"Well, the way it is *supposed* to work is that the workshop is a US workshop. The way it *usually* works is that some of the cats from Milwaukee, or any other city for that matter, tend to step in and try to *reprogram*, for lack of a better phrase, our lady steppers."

"Because they think we are doing it wrong?" I asked.

"Maybe, but I just think it's an ego thing. This particular group in Milwaukee is pretty cool, so CJ seems to think this workshop will be different, but we shall see. The stepping community is the same no matter where you take it, Ginger. Division, conflict, egos, assholes, and money. It's never totally about the dance or having a good time and enjoying the art. There is always an undercurrent of madness. But for some of us, it just adds to our passion for the dance."

"Cam told me that there is no wrong way to step," I said.

"Right," Harper agreed, "that's what makes the dance unique. No two steppers are the same. I think that's what I fell in love with most when I started this journey over three years ago. The creativity and individuality are what make the dance special."

"And it's sexy as hell," I added with a smirk.

"That too."

∽

We finally arrived at the host hotel around nine p.m. Harper and I checked in at the front desk and headed to the suite. On the elevator ride up, I sent Stacey a text letting her know we had made it. My phone rang the minute the elevator doors opened.

"What room are you in?" Vivian asked.

"Four thirty-two," I answered. "Wait, how did you know we were here?"

"Okay, I'm coming to get you."

"Wait, Viv!" I ordered. "We literally just walked into the hotel. Let me put my bags down and grab some comfortable clothes and I will meet you guys at Ivy's. What room is she in?"

"We have two adjoining two-bedroom suites on the third floor. Three twenty-eight and thirty."

"Okay," I said, "see you in about half an hour."

"All right, G, or I will come and get you," Vivian threatened before I hung up.

"Sounds like you're late to the party," Harper said.

"Nah, I think they are doing just fine without me. Besides, Viv is nosey as hell. I hope she doesn't think she's gonna grill me about you in front of a bunch of women."

"I could use a little publicity," Harper joked, popping the collar on his jacket.

"Funny," I said with a smirk, "but I think we agree that

actions speak louder than words, so I say we let folks see what they see—real or imagined."

"Deal," Harper agreed.

I hung my dress for Saturday night and put away a few things from my bag. I quickly grabbed a pair of shorts, a tank top, and some sneakers, since I didn't really know what to expect from a line dance party.

"Thanks for the fun ride and conversation, Harper," I said. "I will see you a little later, okay?"

"For sure," Harper answered.

He kissed me on the cheek and I headed to Ivy's soirée.

⌇

When I made it to the third floor, I could hear the music down the hall from Ivy's suite. I was sure we were going to have security called on us before midnight.

I knocked on the door three times before Vivian finally answered.

"Get in here, girl. We are just starting to learn Ivy's latest creation: 'Love on Top,'" Vivian said as she pulled me through the door.

As I looked around the room, I counted about ten women. Some I recognized from Ivy's line dance class that ended right before the steppers' class began. I gave a hug to Eleana-I'm-here-to-find-a-man, whom I hadn't seen in a while. She started stepping the same time as me and Sasha, but I knew she had recently taken a bigger interest in line dancing. After I said hello to everyone else, I noticed that I didn't see Stacey. Even though I knew she wasn't wild about line dancing, I knew she was in Milwaukee. I sent her a text to let her know I had made it to town and was at Ivy's party with Vivian and the girls.

"Okay, ladies," Ivy began, "let me demo the dance and then we will break it down."

"Ivy started the music and Faith, one of her Dynamic Divas of Dance line dancers, joined Ivy in the demonstration.

The rest of us sat and watched in amazement as the two of them danced in perfect unison to "Love on Top" by Beyoncé. There were a lot of different sequences of steps in the choreography, but it really did look like fun. And as the song played on, I noticed that at some points in the dance, the steps began to repeat themselves. *Hmmm, I might be able to pick this up after all.*

"All right, ladies, let's have a good stiff shot and then take the first two eight counts of the dance," Ivy said amid all the chatter and cackling.

Thank goodness there was wine since I'm not exactly a shot taker. We all took a few minutes to have a drink and a quick snack, and then up we were in two rows of four behind Ivy and Faith.

They walked us through the first two counts of eight of the dance while playing snippets of the music so that we could get a feel for the tempo. In what seemed like no time at all, most of us had the basic dance and were all doing it together. We took breaks here and there to drink, eat, and, of course, gossip a little.

"So, Gigi, how are you liking our little stepping family

so far?" Ivy asked. "You are getting close to about a year, right?"

"About ten months," I replied, "and I really like everything so far. Everyone has been so nice and helpful, and most importantly, patient. The dance is a lot of fun."

"Spoken like a true beginner," a woman I didn't know chimed in.

"Hi, Gigi, I'm Karen," the woman said as she outstretched her hand to shake mine. "I don't want to wreck your positive vibe, but just wait, there is madness to the stepping game."

"Ignore her bitter ass," Ivy interrupted. "If you kept your knees together, you wouldn't even be talking about that mess!"

A loud "ooh" filled the room after Ivy's remark, followed almost immediately by laughter. Karen even snickered, but just a little, along with everyone else. *Definitely more to that story,* I thought.

Vivian confirmed my suspicions when she leaned in and whispered, "I'll fill you in later, G."

Before I knew it, the time was way past midnight. We had all had too much to eat and drink, but had managed to learn exactly two line dances. Even though Harper and I hadn't made any plans, we were staying in the same room, so I thought it was only considerate to send him a text:

Good news, Harper. The bathroom is all yours tonight!☺ Our party is not ending any time soon, so I am going to hang out with Ivy, Viv, and the girls. I will meet you for tea and breakfast and we can head to the workshop together, okay?

He wrote back a few minutes later:
Cool. Have fun and see you in the a.m.

∽

The next morning, I stumbled out of Ivy's suite wearing a tank top, shorts, and no shoes and found my way back to Harper's and my room. I was fumbling at the door with my key, phone, shoes, and handbag all in hand when the door opened.

"This looks like the first day I met you downtown," Harper smiled, wearing nothing but a towel.

"I suppose it does," I said, giving him a remembering look. "Only that day I actually had shoes on, and you were wearing . . . a hat."

"Ha! Looks like you ladies had a good time last night. Give me ten minutes and the bathroom is all yours."

I watched Harper walk toward the bathroom, which was still steamy from his shower. I tried not to stare, but I would be lying if I said I weren't trying to imagine what was going on under that towel. I only caught a glimpse of his chest, but it looked absolutely spectacular.

I sat on the sofa in our suite and checked my phone. I had finally received a reply from Stacey from the text I had sent her last night. She had replied a few hours ago, around six a.m.

Sorry for the late reply, honey. Handling some business. Glad you made it safely. Will see you and Harper @ the workshop.

Ten minutes later, Harper was out of the bathroom like

he promised.

"It's all yours," he said.

"Thank you, sir," I replied.

I grabbed my toiletry bag, went into the bathroom, and shut the door.

∽

When I was finally dressed, Harper and I headed down to the hotel restaurant for breakfast. We had about two hours before the workshop was to start, so there was plenty of time to grab a bite. When we stepped into the dining room, I noticed a few of the women from Ivy's party just sitting down to eat. They did a total double take when they saw Harper and me together. I smiled and they smiled back and then promptly began whispering.

"And now it begins," Harper warned.

We grabbed a seat in a booth by a window.

"So how was the line dancing last night?" Harper asked. "Are you hooked?"

"Maybe," I answered. "It was a good time, and for the most part everyone was pretty cool. And besides that, it is really great exercise."

"Hey, I am all in favor of moving that body," Harper agreed.

"I learned a couple line dances, so I will see if I'm brave enough to get out on that floor tonight," I said. "Hey, how was your night with the fellas?"

"Oh, CJ, Cam, John, and I hung out in the sports bar,

talking about how we were going to arrange the workshop today. Turns out that the brothers think that the class is really ours today and that the regular instructors have agreed to let us teach a few turns and combinations to their students. They claim that they will just be there for support and to reinforce what we are teaching. Hmmm. I'll believe it when I see it," Harper said.

"Hey, it might be exactly as they say," I said. "Either way, I am absolutely sure that I will learn something today!"

"That's the way to think, Ginger," Harper added. "You're right, it will be a good time regardless of who is teaching what to whom."

The waitress arrived at our table. I ordered an egg white omelet with spinach, tomato, and mushrooms, along with a Diet Coke.

"Diet Coke *for breakfast!*" Harper exclaimed, frowning and laughing all at the same time.

He ordered the same thing as I did, adding turkey sausage and hot tea to his order.

"If you have any green tea with ginger, I will take that," Harper smiled at the waitress and then turned that smile to me.

"Besides, you of all people should know by now that I love the smell and taste of *ginger*—in my tea that is."

What a corny remark, but I must have been smiling from ear to ear.

∽

About an hour later, Harper and I pulled up in front of the community center where the workshop was being held.

"You ready?" Harper asked.

"Sure," I answered. "Do you want to walk in together or shall I wait in the car?"

"Very funny, Ginger," Harper snapped. "C'mon, let's go."

As we walked into the building, we could hear CJ's voice resonating down the hallway. When we arrived to the large open room where the workshop was about to begin, Vivian spotted us right away and waved us into the room.

This was different—larger—than I had expected. There were about fifty people in the room. But I was pleasantly surprised that the number of men, most of whom I did not recognize, seemed to equal the number of women in attendance. Already a noticeable difference than the stepping scene in the Twin Cities.

I saw Cam, who gave both Harper and me a thumbs-up when we walked into the room. CJ was speaking alongside two other men; I surmised they were the local instructors, given their places at the front of the class near CJ and Cam.

At this point, I tried not to notice the small group of Untouchable Steppers who had made the trip whispering among themselves. CJ helped to break it up by introducing Harper as another guest instructor.

"Harp here has been stepping with me and Cam for the last three years. He has developed his own style of the dance. For you ladies who don't like many turns but want a nice and smooth dance, you will enjoy stepping with Harp."

Harper took his usual bow as I quietly took my place

in the group of students next to Vivian. It was good to see Stacey, too, as she sat at the door collecting money and workshop participants' contact information.

CJ and Cam split up the class by skill level. Naturally, Eleana and I were with the beginners, but our group was the smallest, which was nice. Using Stacey as their partner, CJ and Cam were demonstrating advanced combinations and connecting turns to the intermediate steppers, while Harper was doing individualized instruction for a few couples who wanted pointers on their dance. The instructor for our group was one of the local Milwaukee instructors, named Ant. Short for Anthony, I think.

Our group of six started out with drills on our basic turns. I was pretty proud of myself that I was able to do all of the turns as Ant called them out by name: right turn, left turn, change of direction, extended right, fake turn. He went down the line giving each of us the signal for each turn to make sure we had the foundation.

"Nice, ladies," Ant began. "Now we are going to dance. I want to see how well you follow without being told what is coming next. You have all just shown me that your foundation is solid; so now is a good time to learn *not* to anticipate. Anticipation hardens your dance and makes it less natural. Let the man have his way with you, and you two will look like you have been dancing together for years."

Why did that sound like an unsavory proposition? I figured I was about to find out what Harper meant about the Mil-town male dancers.

Ant called one of the men from the group that CJ and

Cam were working with to dance with us. The six of us stood in a horizontal line, just as I had done in one of my very first classes with the twins. We had been told to maintain our basic eight-count step to the beat of the music until it was our turn to dance with one of the Milwaukee steppers. As Ant made his way down the line, dancing with each woman for about two minutes, I began to get really nervous. I was third in line, and he was just beginning to dance with the woman next to me. She was from Milwaukee, so I assumed that she had danced with Ant before, but even she stumbled a few times on some of the signals for turns he was giving to her.

My heart was beating a mile a minute when I just happened to glance in Harper's direction. He smiled and nodded as if to say, "You got this," and I felt a little better.

All of a sudden, Ant grabbed me around the waist and spun me into a left turn. I didn't have time to think, which was probably a good thing at that point. Out of the left turn, he immediately gave me an extended right into a reverse. I had only done that turn once with Link, but I was able to catch it, even though a little delayed.

"Nice," Ant complimented.

Next he gave me a left spin and a fake turn. He danced beside me for a while, doing some kind of fancy footwork I had never seen before. Then I was back in front of him and he was moving my arms in a motion resembling me stroking my own hair. I felt silly, and it must have shown on my face.

"See, now you're having fun with it. That's what it's all about."

Ant gave me a right turn, turned simultaneously with me,

gave me a butt bump on the way around, and proceeded to move on down the line to the next victim.

The next hour continued in that fashion. Ant and the other Milwaukee steppers continued to dance with us until we seemed more comfortable and confident in our own skin. It seemed as though he wasn't trying to teach us technical moves, but help us get a feeling of the dance and our partners.

"You all put in work, ladies," Ant said as he applauded our small group. "Outside of the extended with a reverse, I know that we didn't spend much time teaching technical moves, but we still hope you take something away from our time together today. Continue to feel the music, and I think you all are well on your way to becoming natural-born steppers. I will be looking for a dance with each of you at the set tonight."

We had a little time at the end of class to talk, drink water, and snack on fruit and popcorn. CJ and Cam were still giving bits of instruction to some of the class participants. Harper was talking to Ant and a few of the other guys from Milwaukee. Then I saw Stacey walking across the emptying dance floor.

"What did you think of the workshop, honey?" she asked me with a big smile and hug.

"It was good. I think I learned something, but I'm not quite sure what!" I answered. "Hey, where were you last night?" I asked when I remembered she skipped Ivy's party.

"Girl, CJ had me up late working on logistics for the workshop and making sure things were in order for the set." Stacey was speaking quietly and looking around the room as she answered.

"Okay. Well, why didn't you write me back till morning?"

"Just crashed when I was finished around three," Stacey answered me with her head down, still seeming a little nervous and anxious to change the subject. "We will hang out tonight at the set. How was the line dancing?"

"Oh, that was fun too. And interesting. Viv and I need to get you in a corner and tell you all about it."

We both began to whisper as Vivian walked over to break up the conversation.

"Did Gigi tell you about that fool, Karen, at Ivy's party last night?" Vivian chimed in.

"Not yet, but I figured that's who you were talking about. She's harmless, but she is a trip," Stacey added. "This ain't the time or place, you two. We will talk about this when we get back home."

"Where were you last night anyway, Stace?" Vivian asked.

"I was trying to get that question answered myself, Viv," I happily instigated.

"You two are crazy . . . and Ms. Gigi, you have some nerve asking questions. You know I will be interrogating you about Harper. See you back at the hotel," Stacey said as she headed back to the front of the room where workshop participants were beginning to leave.

⚭

"Well, that was fun," I said as Harper held my car door open.

"Yeah, it turned out to be a good workshop," Harper

agreed. "It is always cool when I can add something, even if it's small, to make someone feel like they have improved their dance."

"I know what you mean. I didn't get a lot of technical instruction from Ant today, but dancing with him was a good way for me to start incorporating my own personality into my dance."

"I saw you going to work," Harper said. "Ant said you did a nice job. I told him we had a few privates. He didn't grope you, did he?"

"No!" I yelled. "He was a little suggestive at times, but nothing super inappropriate. He seemed like a nice dude."

"Yeah, they're cool brothers, but everyone has their own style."

"Indeed they do. Say, what was interesting to me, though," I continued, "neither CJ or Cam seemed surprised that the two of us arrived together."

"You know I told them last night that we had come here together. They asked me a few personal questions, to which they received no answers, but I basically told them that you and I are cool, we like each other's company, and that I invited you to check out a set out of town."

"Just like that, huh?" I asked.

"Yep, just like that."

∞

When we made it back to the hotel, Harper and I grabbed a quick salad for supper and got ourselves dressed for the set.

We wanted to get there early because we knew that there would be a live performance by one of our favorite R&B artists, Carmichael MusicLover. His song, "Pot of Gold," was one of my all-time favorite stepping tracks, so I wanted to make it in time for his show.

We arrived at the ballroom where the set was being held. It was a stand-alone building that looked like it had been the spot to be back in its day. It was old but not run down, and was really artistically beautiful inside. It was reminiscent of a time and place where our parents might have gone for a night of live jazz or maybe a doo-wop concert. The tables were small, about four seats around, and pretty tealight candles illuminated the room. There was a small stage strategically placed at the front of the room, and the walls revealed exposed brick and mortar to add some depth and history. It was definitely a classy setup.

As promised, Vivian had saved me a seat at one of the tables near the front of the room.

"Isn't this nice?" she said as Harper pulled out my chair.

"It is really classy," I said, "and you know my decorator instincts are loving all this detail and original architecture."

"Definitely. It's cool that when we come and visit *some* steppers out of town, they treat us to a nice place like this," Vivian started. "I've been to a few spots in Chicago where I felt like I needed a bullet-proof vest!"

We both laughed.

"Want a drink, love?" Harper asked.

"Sure, a glass of anything white, except Chardonnay," I answered. "Thanks, Harper."

"How about you, Vivian?" Harper asked.

"A Coke would be great," Vivian answered. "Thank you."

Harper went to the bar to grab our drinks. Ivy came from behind the stage to let us know that she would be calling us up to perform the line dance we had all learned the night before.

"You both have the dance down, so I want you to get out there and have some fun with it!" Ivy said. "Pretty soon you will be addicted to line dancing just like you are to stepping."

"I'll do my best," I replied. "It won't be hard to have fun with it, Ivy. It's a fun dance. You will have everyone in the room wanting to learn it!"

"That's the plan," Ivy said with a smile.

After about another fifteen minutes, the show began with Ant, our instructor from the workshop earlier, along with a group of the Milwaukee steppers making a few announcements and welcoming visitors. Since we were the largest out-of-town group in attendance, they gave a special shout-out to Untouchable Steppers for joining them in Milwaukee for their fifth anniversary weekend.

"And now coming to the stage is one of Mil-town's favorite line dance divas," Ant started. "She is going to perform some of our favorites and show us one of her new creations! Let's give it up for Ivy and her Dynamic Divas of Dance!"

By now, I was familiar with the cheers that Ivy and her group always elicited from the crowd. They were quite the group to watch. As I was sitting with Eleana waiting to be called up to demonstrate Ivy's "Love on Top," I heard a few women whispering at the table next to me: "She really thinks she is all that!"

What did that mean? And which *she* were they referring to? I quickly decided that it didn't matter. I was too nervous about getting up in front of this crowd to perform a dance I had learned less than twenty-four hours earlier.

"All right, ladies," Ivy said from the stage, "don't make me call you out. You know who you are! Come join me as we share the debut of 'Love on Top!'"

Eleana and I made our way to the floor just in front of the stage. Ivy came down and joined us in the front row with Karen and the rest of her line dance regulars. I was more than happy to be in the back row. The music started and we performed the dance, and I must say that it was just as much fun as it had been the night before. When Ivy invited ladies—and gents—from the audience to join in, I noticed almost immediately that the women whispering at the table next to me were first in line to try to learn Ivy's new creation. I could only interpret that to mean that they must have wanted someone to think that they, too, were *all that*.

When the song ended, Ant was back onstage wasting no time at all. After the last of the line dancers exited the floor, our Milwaukee host was welcoming Mr. MusicLover himself to the stage.

"There he is!" Vivian shouted as she rushed to the front of the stage.

Harper took my hand and we joined other steppers on the dance floor. Then, in the middle of Carmichael's "Go Steppin'," something happened to me on that dance floor that had never happened before. Another man grabbed me away from Harper by the waist and started dancing with me as if he had asked me from the start. Apparently, Harper told me later, it was an acceptable practice as long as the men made eye contact with one another. Let me just say, I was glad that it happened to be Ant, whom I had at least spent time dancing with in our workshop earlier that day.

Once I calmed down from the shock of being stolen away from Harper, Ant and I had a nice dance. He gave me the signals for some of the turns and combinations we had practiced during the workshop. Because it wasn't my first dance with him, I began to relax and start having fun. When the song ended, I thanked Ant for the dance and gave him a big hug. The music for "Pot of Gold" started to play.

"I know this is your track, Ginger," Harper said. "Let's go to work, stepper. Ain't nobody taking you from me on this one."

I smiled, and Harper and I started to dance, really closely. There couldn't have been more than an inch of space between our bodies at any given point. About halfway through the song, he gave me a carousel turn, and suddenly I felt him dipping me slowly and gently all the way to the floor. He held me in that dip for what seemed to be forever. We stared at each other as if we were frozen in that moment. I knew we had been in that position too long when the crowd started to applaud. I didn't know if the applause was for our dip or for Carmichael. Regardless of the reason, the noise brought us out of our trance and we began to dance again.

When the song ended, Harper held my hand and escorted me back to the table. We both spent the rest of the night dancing with the Mil-town crew of men and women, who had been wonderful hosts all weekend. Harper and I didn't dance again that evening, but we both knew that something had happened on that dance floor. I, for one, couldn't wait to find out.

∞

The air was thick in the car on the way back to the hotel. Harper and I were still hot and sweating from so much dancing, so the windows were all the way down.

"Look at your hair blowing all over the place," Harper said. "Want me to put the windows up?"

"No," I answered. "It feels really good."

He looked at me, but he wasn't smiling. "Looks good too," he said with a wink.

The hotel parking lot was pretty full, so Harper pulled up to the entrance to drop me off.

"I'm okay with walking. I'm still so hot!"

"Okay, I hear you. I can't believe how warm it is for October!"

We both smiled.

Harper opened my car door and took my hand. We walked into the hotel and hopped into the elevator. Harper stood behind me with his arms around my waist. I could feel his wet body pressed against me from his chest all the way down to his thighs.

We only had four floors to go, but it felt like an eternity. I closed my eyes for a minute and exhaled. I didn't think it was possible for this man to smell any better—and wringing wet with sweat on top of it!

Finally the fourth floor. Harper unlocked the door to our room.

"Want some tea?" he asked.

Hell no I don't want no goddamn tea! Well, that's what I wanted to say, but a polite "No thanks" is what came out.

"I could use a glass of water, though," I said, "and I need to get out of these wet clothes."

"I can help you with both of those. What do you want first?"

Before the word *first* made it all the way out of his mouth, our lips were pressed against each other like they had been craving it all night. We had kissed several times before, but this time was somehow different, and the passion of the moment completely swept us away.

After a few minutes, Harper backed away and looked into my eyes. I could almost hear what he was thinking: We have waited all of these months, so why rush it now?

I couldn't agree more.

He took my hand and led me to the bench at the foot of the bed. He took off my shoes and kissed each of my toes one by one. He rubbed my ankles, calves, and thighs underneath my dress, giving me little kisses all along the way. He was gonna have to peel me off the ceiling after a few more minutes of this.

When he leaned in close enough for a kiss, I unbuttoned his shirt that was totally stuck to his body. He helped me pull it off along with his T-shirt. *Damn,* I thought as I looked at that chest of his. He reached around my back and unzipped my dress. He helped me stand as it fell to the floor.

"Damn," he said, as he started kissing my neck. He opened the clasp of my bra and worked his lips down to my breasts. His hands were wonderful. I could feel them constantly caressing some part of my body. I learned long ago to never underestimate the power of touch when it comes to intimacy. If we had fallen asleep in each other's arms at that moment, I would have been totally satisfied.

I don't believe that any more than you do.

Still kissing with purpose, I started to walk toward the bed, but Harper redirected me to the work desk near the dresser of drawers. He lifted me up onto the desk and positioned his body high between my thighs. By now, the sweat on our skin had mixed into this sensual aroma of sweetness and heat.

Harper removed my black lace panties and dropped to his knees. Within seconds my hands were behind me, pressed against the desk, and my back was arched in esctasy.

Once he was back to his feet, I wrapped my legs around his waist and pulled him closer. As we started to kiss again, I unbuckled the belt on his pants and he let them fall to the floor. Even his boxers were cute, but it was time for them to go.

He lifted me off the desk with my legs still around his waist and placed me on the bed. He stroked my hair with his hand and kissed me softly in a style characteristic only of a true gentleman.

"You are so wet," Harper whispered in my ear.

I closed my eyes, pulled him in deeper, and melted into him. His hands, lips, and body moved in harmony with every inch of my frame. The feeling was indescribable. There was something about his rhythm.

We fell asleep still wrapped in each other's arms. I think I remember waking up once in the middle of the night with my head on his chest, happy to learn that I hadn't been dreaming.

∽

The morning after was quiet. We dressed quietly. We shared a quiet breakfast with a quiet cup of tea. We quietly packed up the car as we got ready to leave Milwaukee.

"Okay, I am just going to say it. My G-spot made a new friend last night!"

"Wow . . . so much for being worried about *breaking* the ice this morning," Harper said. "Thanks for *smashing* it!"

We both started to laugh a little as we were merging onto the highway headed home.

"But now that you mention it," Harper started, "wow, you are really in tune with your body, Ginger."

"Sure, but not with just anyone, Harper," I admitted. "And you are rather skilled, I might add."

"Thank you very much, madame," Harper said, smiling. "I do take pride in my talent. Ordinarily I would take a bow, but I am driving."

Somehow I knew he wasn't joking.

"Seriously, though, first things first," Harper said in a thoughtful tone. "I apologize for being so irresponsible. I know we have known each other going on almost a year now, but we have never really discussed one anothers' *history* or anything like that. So please forgive me for getting caught up in the moment and not taking precautions the way I should have."

"Nice," I said, "and I appreciate your apology. I could say the same thing to you about the irresponsibility thing, but I do feel as though I have gotten to know you pretty well over these last nine or ten months. Neither of us is a virgin, but neither of us is promiscuous either. Adult relationships come with baggage, and I think that we are both pretty level-headed. If there was something one of us needed to know, caught up in the moment or not, I am confident that we would have said what needed to be said."

"Cool," Harper said. "I appreciate your understanding. But I have to say, that shit was hot! Let's just be real . . . our connection existed long before we ever reached the bedroom. Truth be told, I guess we have been making love for months on the dance floor. I know how your body moves, and I know how to move in perfect sync with it."

He was so dreamy when he talked like that.

"Now back to these orgasms," Harper continued.

So much for the dreaminess. I spoke too soon.

"But damn, girl, it bears repeating, you really are in tune with your body. And forgive the candor, but your sugar walls . . . ooowee! Sweet! You, Gabrielle Ginger Grant, have the sweetest—"

"Stop right there, Harper Drake! Don't you dare finish that sentence! Oh my goodness!" was all I could screech as I put my head in my hands.

"Wow—you are turning a shade of red I don't think I've ever seen! Don't ever be ashamed of the truth!" Harper said, relishing in my embarrassment.

"Just drive, crazy man." I smiled as I pointed to the high-way sign reading "Minneapolis."

✍ *Chapter Seventeen*

The change of seasons was in full bloom. We were well into autumn, and the holidays would soon be at our doorstep once more. What a difference a year makes. Harper and I had been officially dating for about a month now, and I would soon be celebrating my one-year anniversary of this dance called steppin'.

✍

It was a warm late October morning. Stacey and I had agreed to meet at the lake for a run. Over the years, she and I had tried just about every conceivable workout that was most popular at the time. Core pilates, kickboxing, hot yoga, and spinning, to name a few. At the end of it all, each time we would take up running once again. The one element that remained consistent during our workouts was that we always managed to have full-blown conversations, regardless of the type of exercise endeavor we were engaged in at the time. Makes me wonder how strenuous any of those activities actually were.

During our run, naturally I had to share a few crucial details from the Milwaukee road trip, giving Stacey specifics about me and Harper that I could only share with her. I

changed the subject and started chatting it up about the girls
and their extracurriculars that were just getting underway
a few months into the school year. I was in the middle of
making fun of the tone-deaf soloists featured in Isabel's last
choir concert when I was stopped clean in my tracks by a
screaming voice.

"Oh my God, Gigi! I can't keep it a secret any longer!"
Stacey cried hysterically.

As I held her in my arms, trying to console her to no
avail, I asked again and again, "What is it, Stacey? What's
going on?"

After what seemed like hours had passed, Stacey was finally able to catch her breath. We sat on the bench a mile
into our run, and she began to tell me how she had fallen in
love with CJ.

∞

I already knew that CJ and Stacey had met almost five
years ago when she first started dancing. What I didn't know
was a year after that, her marriage was on the rocks, she
was in the middle of a career change, and her parents were
splitting up.

"It was a really tough time for me, Gigi," my friend began. "Mom and Dad were separating after forty years of
marriage. Greg was in and out of town every week, trying to
get the start-up law firm off the ground. I was left with the
kids day in and day out with no support. You know how that
can wear on you."

"Of course," I said.

"I was already so miserable about moving to another state and uprooting our family from the home we know and the people we love," Stacey continued. "And do you remember what I was going through at that time with the firm? I was on the verge of leaving and starting my own publicist business. Everything was a mess. But my one bright spot was serving on my first nonprofit board for Communities United. It was important work that had meaning, and I could offer my resources and skills to help promote activities and events in the community. I felt useful and in control when I was doing that work. And that is where I met Carter Justice."

Stacey went on to share the story of a happy hour one night after a board meeting to toast one of the member's birthdays. Although it was an eight-member board of directors, by the end of the night, she and CJ were the only two left at the table.

"He was so charismatic. I admired his ideas and creativity. We hit it off right away and knew that we would be able to work together on event planning. Naturally he told me about his organization, Untouchable Steppers, and encouraged . . . well, convinced, me to take his class," Stacey said. "He told me that the only way I could successfully publicize his events was to become a part of the organization and really develop a love and appreciation for the dance."

"Was he right?" I asked.

"I don't know if he was right, but I believed him," Stacey continued. "It was easy to confide in him and tell him about everything that I was struggling with at the time. He told me that dancing would be a positive outlet for me with so much negativity swirling around in my life. I took him up on his offer, started classes a few weeks later, and have never looked back."

Stacey told me the story of her first month of classes. Very similar to mine. Like me, she missed several classes in the beginning due to childcare issues combined with Greg's increasing business travel. CJ offered to give her private lessons so that she could continue to learn. At the time, her kids were small, and so she often invited CJ to her home. Their private lessons started after the kids were put to bed.

"Well, you don't have to tell me the rest of *that* story." I smirked.

"Gigi, I don't know how I let that happen, but once I did, I didn't know how to stop it!" Stacey admitted.

"Why didn't you come to me?" I asked. "You know I would have done anything to help you through all of this."

"I know, Gigi, but that was the time when you were fighting your ex in court about child support and you were struggling to keep your house," Stacey reminded me. "I couldn't add to all of that when you were trying to be there for your own family."

"Right, but still, Stacey, an affair? I am the last person to judge you because I know how hard life can get, and anything that feels good is easy when you're in the middle of a crisis," I said. "But I have to ask. Does Greg know?"

"I'm still dancing, Gigi," Stacey said. "Of course Greg doesn't know. When we moved to Charlotte, I thought that would be the opportunity we needed to put our marriage back on track and forget about CJ and everything that happened. And it worked. The new business was stressful for him, but because I really hadn't established myself in business circles in Charlotte, I was able to be there one hundred percent of the time for Greg and the kids. The move was good for us."

"But now you're back," I stated the obvious.

"Right," Stacey said.

"So . . . does this mean it is still going on? Between you and CJ, I mean?" I asked directly.

"I will say that we have not crossed the line since we moved back to Minneapolis last year. But we do have our moments. Like in Milwaukee . . . or the night of his birthday party when he and Link had that silly fight. I love my husband, and since we have been back from Charlotte, Greg is attentive and caring and the man I met and married almost ten years ago now. But, CJ, I can't explain it. Our relationship isn't defined by any ordinary standards of what things *should* be. It just *is*, and I can't say more than that."

"Wait—Milwaukee?" I was lost. "The road trip? That *business* you had to take care of . . . why you missed Ivy's party and didn't text me until morning, that was CJ?"

"Partly," Stacey admitted.

"What's the other part?" I needed to know.

"Remember at the workshop when Viv mentioned Karen and that she was acting a fool at the line dance party? I said to you both that she was a trip, but we would have to talk about that later. Remember?"

"Vaguely," I said, trying to recall. "Wait, she was the one

Ivy called *bitter* and said something about her keeping her legs together."

"That would be Karen," Stacey concluded. "Well, I couldn't come to Ivy's party because I knew Karen would be there. To put it mildly, she does not care for me at all. CJ broke her heart, and she blames me for his decision to end things with her. She stopped stepping and now she only line dances."

"Wait, how many—?" I stopped myself. "Nevermind, I don't even want to finish that question. Aren't you worried if Karen suspects your relationship with CJ that others in the circle do too?"

"CJ and I are very discreet. And above everything else, we are close friends. He is not expecting me to abandon my family, and I know that he is not at a place in his life where he wants to settle down. I guess my outburst today was a result of my need to tell someone the truth because I have been keeping this secret for almost five years."

"But you screamed a few minutes ago that you love him," I reminded her.

"And I do," Stacey said, "but not in the sense that you think. CJ and I have a supportive relationship that we both benefit from. He knows that I am committed to my marriage, and I know that he sees other women. But at the end of the day, we know that we will always be there for one another."

"Wow" was all I could muster.

Typical Stacey trying to conduct a cost-benefit analysis of the situation. She was still trying to be the consummate businesswoman.

"I know, I know, it's a lot. But I trust you like a sister, and I know that you will not tell a soul."

"Are you kidding, Stace?" I asked. "Never."

I didn't have the heart to tell her that I wish she hadn't told me either.

∽

"So how was your run this morning?" Harper asked as he pulled out a stool for me at his kitchen counter.

"Good," I replied.

"How many times did you two make it around the lake?"

"Yep," I answered.

"Oh yeah, well I ran today too. It was so hot that I had to run totally naked. But I got my ten miles in and managed to avoid getting arrested."

"That's great, Harper," I said. "Wait . . . what?"

"Okay, Ginger," Harper said, interrupting my daze, "what's going on? Clearly your head is elsewhere. Is everything okay?"

"I think so." I smiled a little after he repeated what he had just told me.

"I got some news earlier and I'm not quite sure what to make of it," I said.

"I'm a good listener," Harper offered.

"You certainly are," I agreed. "When I am ready to share, you will be the first to know. It's girl stuff, you know. And I just need to process and be supportive at this point."

"Girl stuff, huh?" Harper smirked. "Is that another way to say gossip?"

"How dare you!" I pretended to be offended. "Not at all. Well, at least not this time. Like I said, I just need a little time to process things. It will work out one way or the other."

"Cool." Harper winked as he took a sip of his tea.

"Let's change the subject," I suggested. "When are we gonna practice again? It's been quite awhile. Come to think of it, I haven't had a private lesson from you since you punked out and I started going to Link's classes back in August."

"Hmm. Punked out, huh?" Harper repeated. "Well, call it what you want. I was trying to keep the peace. Anyway, we can practice whenever you want. *Link*," Harper continued with a smirk, "I'm surprised he didn't ask you to be his new dance partner!"

I turned my head away from Harper, pretending to notice something outside the window.

"Wait," Harper noticed my phony diversionary tactic. "Did he . . . really, Gigi?"

"It was at the end of my third class with him and he told me about a beginner/instructor contest in Chicago in January. He asked me to think about it," I said.

"Yeah, there is one big problem with that," Harper surmised. "You are NOT his student. I should have known when I saw him grab you at the twins' party. You hadn't even started taking his classes yet, and he was twirling you around like you two had been dancing for years."

"Okay," I said. "I never seriously considered it, but I admit that I was flattered. Just out of curiosity, since you clearly know more than I do, whose student am I?"

I couldn't wait to hear this answer.

"You are certainly not Link's student after three classes. That much I know. Everyone knows, the twins included, that I am teaching you how to step," Harper concluded with some authority.

"Yes, sir." I tried to lighten the mood. He had gotten so serious.

"Besides that, do you think you are ready to compete that soon?" Harper asked. "You haven't even been dancing for a year, but he thinks he can get you ready in a few months, huh?"

"It's no big deal, Harper," I said. "But, as my self-proclaimed instructor, I think you are better equipped to answer the question as to whether or not I am *ready* to compete. I'm sure I might be a little nervous, but more than that, I am clearly a beginner and am not sure that it makes sense for me at this level. I don't have folks knocking on my door asking me to be their dance partner. I thought it was nice of him."

"Don't be naïve, Ginger," Harper started. "He wants to get into your pants, plain and simple. I don't mean to be crass, but Link's reputation is not limited to the dance floor. You could talk to quite a few ladies about their escapades with him and how badly they ended. That is how the twins are able to keep so many of his female students once they leave his classes."

"You sure do know a lot," I interrupted. "All those grinning women confiding in you, huh?"

"Of course not," Harper answered. "But in this small circle, you hear things and the twins talk—especially after they get a student of Link's who has left his classes for personal reasons."

"I think it goes both ways," I interrupted. "I learned that Lena and Rocco started with the twins."

"Right. But I really think that was a personality issue," Harper said. "Who really knows? These cats are all in it for the wrong reason, if you ask me. It is never just about the dance and having a good time."

"So, let's just drop it," I suggested. "We are wasting our time together talking about things that don't really matter. But, still a little bit on topic, once the holidays are over, the twins' big annual contest will be back before you know it. Do you have someone in mind this year?"

"Several women have asked me, but I really haven't given it much thought at all. I can tell you it won't be Eva, but beyond that, I haven't even decided if I am participating this year."

"I just thought I would ask while we were on the subject," I said. "Last year during our first all-nighter, I remember you telling me how hard it is to have a dance partner that you have no personal connection with."

"Right," Harper confirmed.

"Well, maybe that's why you haven't won a contest yet, Mr. Drake," I said with a big smile. "You haven't had a dance partner who was also your one and only."

"I thought we were changing the subject." Harper laughed as he smacked my backside.

"Finally a smile," I said. "You were so serious for a minute there."

∞ *Chapter Eighteen*

For days, I couldn't quite shake either of the conversations I had had with Stacey or Harper. I had definitely struck a nerve with that one. What was I supposed to do with Stacey's confession? What was it about this dance? Twice in a single day—over the course of a few hours really—I had heard about not one, not two, but three of these so-called *leaders* in the stepping community who had been involved with more than one woman in this tiny circle—one of whom just happened to be my closest friend. And let's not forget my new love interest. Admittedly, his confession left me less staggered than Stacey's, but it was still pretty amazing. It seemed like the only one exercising any caution and good sense around here was Vivian, as unlikely as that was. After all, she had always told me to be careful and not to trust any of these steppers.

"You know everyone has a past, Gigi," Vivian reasoned as I told her about Harper's sketchy involvement with some female steppers. "This must be old news because I have never heard anything about it. Like I told you from the beginning, Harper's always been nice to me, and outside of dancing, I had never seen him with a woman."

"It's all good," I said. "I wasn't upset by anything he told me, but I was a little surprised. And I don't want to be in the middle of any mess with any women thinking I took something from them."

"I don't know why you're so surprised. Harper seems like a classy dude, and he's not tough to look at. That's what women are attracted to—that's what you were attracted to, right? Be glad that he at least told you the truth so you can be prepared if mess does come your way," Vivian added. "And like he told you, everyone can see that you two are a couple and out in the open, so he must not have anything to hide."

As always, Vivian had a point. Harper was turning out to be a good guy. But I still wanted to pick her brain about this crazy dynamic with so many women and so few men.

"You knew that before you started the dance, Gigi. And if you didn't, you had to know that there would be some coochie-related drama from Ivy's party alone. You heard Ivy tell Karen she needed to keep her knees together. Rumor has it that Karen used to sleep with CJ."

I couldn't dare tell Vivian that I knew the whole sordid story and that Stacey was a part of it too. Stacey would kill me, and I couldn't take a chance that the story would leak. Vivian was a bit of a talker.

"Really?" I tried to sound surprised.

"Hell yeah, girl. I'm sure the twins could have any of these women that they want. I ain't gonna lie. If Cam came at me like that, he could have me hook, line, and sinker."

"Yes, I know," I interrupted. "You have been perfectly clear about that fact. That's why the man is terrified of you!"

We both laughed.

"Speaking of your men," I started, "how is Mr. DJ?"

"Girl, I had to dump his sorry ass," Vivian said.

"What happened?" I asked.

"Remember when I told you that I thought he was seeing other people and lying to me about it?"

"Yes," I answered.

"Turns out he wasn't. It was the opposite. He was ending all of his other relationships and asked me and the kids to move in with him."

"What?" I could hardly contain my laughter.

"Girl, yes," Vivian continued. "That shit scared the hell outta me. I told him that I was not ready for that kind of commitment and he could check back with me in about a year. By that time, I might have gotten all of my other sources of *entertainment* out of my system."

"A mess," I said. "But that's what happens when a man gets caught up in the enchantment that is Vivian."

"You know it and I know it, and he had to learn it today!" Vivian said as she snapped her fingers in the air.

∽

A week later was the last class before the start of the holiday season, and the twins were inviting everyone to attend their upcoming holiday set being held on one of those Saturday nights in early December right between Thanksgiving and Christmas. Now that Harper and I were dating, I decided it was time I go back to class with the twins. But no matter how hard I tried, I felt as though I were somehow looking at CJ differently now that I knew what had happened between him and Stacey. Stacey had a board meeting, so she wasn't in class. Harper had a late showing, so I was meeting him later. But it was good to see Sasha back in class. I knew that she had been going through some personal issues in her marriage, so I wanted to check on her and see how she was planning to spend her holidays.

"What was with that look you were giving CJ?" Sasha asked.

I guess my sideways glares at CJ weren't as undetectable as I thought.

"Dang, girl, I haven't seen you in over a month and that's your greeting?" I was trying to changing the subject.

Sasha smiled through her laughter. "Sorry, honey, how are you?"

"I'm all right. What are you doing tonight?" I asked.

"Headed home to do laundry," Sasha said.

"C'mon, let's go get that drink we keep talking about and then we can catch up," I suggested.

Sasha left her car at the community center, and I drove the two of us to a bar a few miles away where we could talk.

"How are you really doing?" I asked Sasha as I sipped my cosmopolitan.

"I am getting through," Sasha replied.

Sasha told me that she had filed for legal separation from her husband.

"He told me that he just *lost interest*," she continued.

"Well, what the hell does that mean?" I asked.

"Gigi, hell if I know," Sasha answered. "Truth be told, I was a little bit pissed off 'cause he said it as if he is the most interesting person on the planet!'"

We giggled a little, but I knew she was hurting.

"I am past the point of blaming myself and am just ready to move on with my life, with or without him. I am not even sure that I want to work things out. Besides, he would actually have to make an equal effort to do that, and I don't see that happening in any way, shape, or form."

"Don't rush anything," I advised. "You never know. Men and midlife crises can be something else. At least he wasn't cheating on you . . . was he?"

"He says that there is no one else, but I am not sure that I believe that either. I don't know what to believe anymore. One minute I am thinking about counseling, and the next I am thinking of calling it quits. You've been here, Gigi. What can you tell me?"

"Everyone is different, Sasha, but the one consistency is to trust your instincts. You married this man for a reason, and it's not in our nature to just give up. But it's also not worth it to feel unloved and disrespected. Give it some time, and suddenly one day you will know exactly what to do. Praying don't hurt neither."

"Neither does drinking!" Sasha said as she raised her glass.

We talked for another hour or so before I drove Sasha back to her car and we both headed home. Why was it that when my relationship finally seemed to be going so well, everyone around me seemed to be in utter turmoil? I wished that Sasha weren't going through this, especially at the holidays, but as a casualty of divorce myself, I certainly understood that sometimes the difficult decision was still the best decision. Although she was a relatively new acquaintance, I really liked and admired Sasha as a person. She was strong, down to earth, and had a great spirit about her. Besides that, she was my absolute favorite person to speculate, analyze, and share in steppers' drama, since we were both pretty new to the scene. When I invited her to share Thanksgiving dinner with me and the girls, and Harper, too, she told me she would bring the turkey and homemade cranberry sauce. That's when I knew for sure that we were on our way to becoming great friends.

∞ *Chapter Nineteen*

Thanksgiving had come and gone and Christmas was just a few weeks away. It was the weekend of the twins' holiday set, and I was ready to dance. Harper and I had been practicing at home and in class, but it had been awhile since I had been on a dance floor, so I was looking forward to trying out some of our new moves. I hadn't seen Sasha since our potluck Thanksgiving dinner, so I was looking forward to connecting with her, too.

Harper and I arrived at the twins' holiday set just before ten. The room was beautifully decorated in silver and gold, which, of course, was the holiday color scheme for the evening. It wasn't very crowded, but we had arrived a little early to make sure I had a seat. Sasha had sent me a text a few minutes earlier to let me know she was on her way, so I placed my handbag and fan at a table, and Harper led me to the dance floor.

By the time Harper and I finished dancing to two songs, Sasha had arrived and was sitting at the table where I had placed my bag and fan. At the start of another song, Harper grabbed the hand of another stepper while I headed back to the table to greet Sasha.

"How you doing tonight, sweetie?" I asked, giving Sasha a big hug.

"Pretty good. Thanks again for sharing your family with me at Thanksgiving. It was so much fun hanging out with you and the girls. Harper seems cool too," Sasha said.

"The pleasure was all mine," I said with a smile. "Good food, good friends—that's what it's all about."

"Nice one," a man said as he snapped our picture at the table.

"I'm Zachary," he said, shaking both my and Sasha's hands. "I'm filling in for the regular photographer tonight. You two take a great picture together. Let me get one more."

Sasha and I put our heads together and smiled for the handsome photographer.

"Thanks," he said.

"Thank you," Sasha said.

Zachary turned and walked away with a big smile.

While the line dancers took the floor for three or four songs, Harper went to buy me a glass of wine, and Sasha and I sat and watched the group do a line dance called "Tambourine." Looked like I would be able to learn that one after a few rounds, but I didn't want to push my luck. I had managed to get through Ivy's "Love on Top" earlier that night without crashing and burning, so I decided I would do a little chair dancing instead, moving my feet while sitting.

"C'mon, let's go try it!" Sasha said.

"Oh no," I said, "but you go ahead, honey. I'll be cheering you on from here."

I continued to try to pick up the moves from my chair as Sasha headed to the dance floor to give the "Tambourine" a try.

"You looked great out there with Ivy and the group. We

steppers aren't going to lose you to line dancing, are we?" It was Link who had taken a seat behind me.

"How are you?" I asked with a smile.

"I'm good. Been missing you in class, but I know how busy you are," Link said.

"The holidays, you know. And besides, taking privates works better sometimes with my schedule," I said, seeing no reason to tell Link I was back in class with Harper and the twins.

"I hear you," Link said. "Hey, I am happy to take some time out and give you a lesson or two if you are interested. I haven't forgotten about that proposition I made the last time you attended my class."

"What proposition was that?" Harper interrupted after placing my glass of wine on the table.

"What's up, Harp!" Link said as he stood to shake Harper's hand.

"What's going on, man?" Harper asked.

"Not much, not much. Good to see you, man."

"No doubt. Now that I think about it, I haven't seen you since the brothers' birthday set in July," Harper said with a twisted lip.

Was he trying to bring up that crazy pseudo-fight from last summer?

"Sometimes that's how it goes, man, but it's all good. My money works at the front door same as everybody else's," Link replied. "Besides, man, you know you're always welcome at my class just like Gigi."

Harper's facial expression instantly changed to one of slight disgust.

"Gigi here tell you that I asked her to be my dance partner next month?" Link continued. "She's a real natural, and I thought she would get a kick out of an instructor/student contest in the Chi."

"Yeah, she told me something about that," Harper replied. "Cool offer, dude, but Gigi is *my* dance partner. We just made that move and are waiting to announce after the new year, so I appreciate you keeping it quiet, bro."

I am?

"Oh." Link was startled. "No problem, man—you two will look good on the floor together."

"Thanks, man," Harper said.

"Grab you later for a dance, Gigi," Link said as he walked away.

"Um" was all I could say.

"Sorry about that, love," Harper said, "but it was the first thing that came out of my mouth."

"Well, I certainly won't hold you to it, Harper," I said. "I totally understand that you had an immediate testosterone-related need to piss on your territory."

He looked at me with a raised brow.

"You never know, Ginger," Harper said. "There just might be something to this *one-and-only* theory of yours. Maybe we should test it out."

Me in a contest? I thought. I didn't say a word. I took Harper's hand as we headed back to the dance floor.

∽

During one of my breaks, I went to the bar for another glass of wine while Harper and Sasha were both on the dance floor. As I was tipping the bartender, I noticed DeAnn, the leader of the Furious Five, walking toward me.

"Gigi, right?" she asked.

"Yes," I answered. "You are DeAnn, right?"

"That is correct," she answered. "I know we haven't officially met, but I just wanted to let you know that we have had our eyes on you and Harper ever since we saw you dance at Link's set a few months back."

Where in the hell is this conversation going? I thought.

"We think we like you two together," DeAnn said. "In fact, we like it a lot. We don't usually get in people's personal business, but we thought you would want to know that we think you and Harper make a nice couple. Harper has always been respectful to us, so it is nice to see him with a good girl and not one of these round-the-way hoes."

"Well, thank you so much, DeAnn," I tried to answer sincerely. "I really appreciate the compliment."

I think it was a compliment.

"Anytime, sugar," she said. "Come and meet the rest of the girls sometime soon, okay?"

"I will do that as soon as I am done with my next dance," I answered as I saw Link headed my way to collect on the dance he promised earlier.

Just then I looked over DeAnn's shoulder, and the remaining four of the Furious Five were all smiling and waving their hands at me.

I waved back. What do you know? I think that meant I had

just received a stamp of approval from the Five. Maybe they considered it to be their Christmas gift to me. Regardless of the reason, like I said before, those Five were totally harmless in my eyes. But I had absolutely no doubt that once I took a little time to get to know them, the collection of stories they would have to share would be undeniably fascinating.

∽

The holidays were truly joyous, but they had gone by so quickly. I was already seeing off my mother and sister, who had come for a visit at Christmas, which was shortly followed by a trip to the airport sending my girls to visit their dad for the second week of their holiday break. Sasha and I had been spending more time together, Christmas shopping and hanging out at the spa, but I also made sure to include her in our all-girls holiday so that she didn't have to spend much time alone. She didn't have any children, so she always got a kick out of the antics between Grace and Isabel. Aside from that, Sasha was a great cook and, even better still, she gave my mother another pair of ears to talk into oblivion.

The weather had been brutal in the Twin Cities this winter. Temperatures were double digits below normal for this time of the year, and school had been canceled for days at a time. Harper had spent Christmas in Detroit with his family, but he was headed back home to ring in the new year with me. I was glad that we had gotten a break in the current wave of blizzards so that his plane could land safely at home.

"Did you miss me?" Harper asked as he removed his coat.

"Of course," I said, brushing the snow from his hat. "I'm so glad the weather didn't keep you away."

"Nah, but I do wish the roads were a little better so that the New Year's Eve party hadn't been cancelled," Harper said.

"Yeah, but it's just the same," I started. "A quiet start to this new year somehow seems appropriate," I said.

I tuned in to our favorite Pandora station and pulled a bottle of champagne from the freezer.

"This music is hot, babycakes," Harper said as he spun in his usual circle. "We can step in the kitchen after midnight . . . our first dance of the new year."

"Romantic," I said with a wink.

"We might as well start practicing now. We only have about ten weeks till the contest."

"You're still on that kick, huh?" I asked.

"Hell yeah! We are going to *do this*!" Harper said.

"You still have time to find another partner, Harper," I said. "I'm a beginner and I saw that contest last year. There's no way—"

"It's four minutes, Ginger," Harper interrupted. "That few minutes in time goes by so quickly that it won't even feel as if we danced to an entire song. I know that this is all new to you and you're probably nervous, but trust me. I know your dance and what you are capable of doing better than anyone, maybe even you! And I can get us where we need to be to make a more than respectable showing."

"I just don't want to let you down, Harper," I admitted. "I remember that look on your face when you and Eva didn't win last year. It was not a look I want to see on your face because of something I did or didn't do."

"Totally different situation, love," Harper started. "First of all, that look on my face was disappointment with myself; it wasn't because of anything Eva did or didn't do. Second, there is no comparison. I am teaching you the eight count so that it fits with my style. Our dance vibes with our flow as a couple."

"How many points can we get for being cute?" I asked, sort of joking.

"Funny," Harper said.

"I am *not* joking," I said, trying not to smile.

"We're just gonna get out there and have fun. I promise," Harper reassured.

Harper removed the cork from the bottle of champagne as the countdown started. We kissed at midnight and then headed to the kitchen for our first dance of the new year.

∾ *Chapter Twenty*

It was the start of another year. I had made new friends, I was in a good relationship, and I had found a new way to express myself through dance. Since Harper and I had made our "partnership" official, we had been practicing at both his place and mine, trying to prepare for this competition which was now only six weeks away. We were still attending class, and both Cam and CJ were totally encouraging and supportive of our decision to enter as a couple.

"The twins are so happy that you guys are entering the contest," Stacey said one evening at class. "CJ told me that you two might really have a chance because you guys bring something new and fresh to the floor. He said that, up until now, Harper has always danced with someone the twins taught and picked for him, which means they are obviously acknowledging the fact that Harper is teaching you the dance."

"That's cool of them," I said, "but I don't need any added pressure. Are they expecting us to win?"

"Relax, honey," Stacey started. "They just think you two look *right* together on that dance floor. No pressure."

"Well good, because as long as I don't wipe out or lose my count, that's pretty much all I'm hoping for at this point," I said with some seriousness. "But how are you doing, Stacey?"

"Good," Stacey answered. "Our holiday ski trip was fabulous. Just me and Greg reconnecting. Still, it's good to be back in the swing of things."

"You know what I'm really asking," I said. "How are *things?*"

"Fine, honey," Stacey started as she took my arm and walked me a little farther away from the door of the class.

"CJ and I are cool," Stacey continued. "Stop worrying. I just needed to confide in you. I told you a few minutes ago that Greg and I had a great trip together."

"I know, but . . ."

"But nothing," Stacey interrupted. "It's all good, Gigi. Focus on Harp, and ya'll be your cute and sexy selves on that dance floor."

"Cute points! I knew they existed!" I said as Harper walked out of the room where class was ending.

"You knew what existed?" Harper nosily interrupted.

"Nothing," Stacey said. "Now you take care of my girl here and don't get all drill sergeant on her, Harper Drake."

"I am always a perfect gentleman," Harper said with silly sincerity.

We all laughed as Stacey headed back into the room. As Harper and I turned to leave class that night, I couldn't help but wonder if Stacey was being honest with me, or with herself for that matter. I hoped she and Greg were really back on track, but she was still so intertwined with stepping and with CJ that I wondered if she would ever be truly free of him, or if she even wanted to be.

⤜⤜

I couldn't believe that it had already been an entire year since I first attended a steppers' contest. What was even harder to believe was that I was about to be a participant in less than forty-eight hours. What was I thinking? Why did I let Harper talk me into this?

"Relax, Gigi," Sasha said as if she could read my thoughts.

"How did you know?" I asked, looking at her in the bathroom mirror of the Westin hotel.

"I can see it all over your face," Sasha answered. "You and Harper look fantastic together. Get out there and do exactly what you said you were going to do: have a good time. I see you two dance more than most, and you can see your connection on the floor. Just be yourselves and it will be easy."

"Why are you always so calm?" I asked sarcastically.

"Because this is a *dance* contest, Gigi," Sasha added. "What is there to get worked up about? I understand nerves and all, but your livelihood isn't at stake. After you dance for three or four minutes or whatever it is, and you walk off that dance floor, you have a life to live. It is just not as serious as others try to make it out to be. Get out there and make sweet love to your man on that dance floor!"

"You are so crazy, Sasha!" I squealed. "But also one hundred percent right."

We were still laughing as we walked up the stairs into the "Welcome to the Twin Cities" set. It was the first night of the three-day weekend of events.

"Let me get a picture of you two," said a woman holding a camera.

"Got it," she said as she snapped a photo of me and Sasha.

"My name is Dolores," she said, extending her hand, "but please call me Dolly. I've seen you a few times before, but we've never met. I have a few nice shots of you and Harper on the dance floor."

"Hi, I'm Gigi, and this is Sasha," I said. "Nice to meet you, Dolly. I think I have seen some of your handiwork on Facebook."

"That's definitely true," Dolly said with a smile. "The twins asked me to take pictures this weekend, so I will see you around the sets. Oh! And that's my husband, Donnie, on the DJ stand tonight. I will introduce you guys to him later on."

"Okay," I said. "I've heard him play before. He's one of my favorites."

"He's the best DJ in the Twin Cities, if you ask me," Dolly whispered. "But I guess I am a little bit biased, too," she added with a giggle. "See you guys later."

Sasha and I headed to our table. Vivian and Stacey both had seats there, but, as usual, they were busy with Untouchable Steppers business and making sure things were going as planned. There was also a seat for Harper and one for Greg, Stacey's husband, who was supposed to come out tonight for the opening event. Stacey told me that Greg was trying to show some interest in her activities outside of the home so that they could continue to build on their relationship. She seemed happy at the prospect of Greg coming out to support her and, under the circumstances, I thought it would be good for this crowd to see Stacey with someone other than CJ.

A few hours passed and Greg had arrived, but there was no sign of Harper. I sent him a text to check on him with no reply. Sasha and I had already been on the dance floor with a few locals as well as some out-of-town guests. I had even braved a few line dances with Eleana and Ivy by my side. The twins acted as cohosts of the event, interrupting now and again to thank the attendees and to provide logistics for the calendar of events over the next few days.

After an announcement about the workshops over the next two days, DJ Donnie started to play a smooth slow tune.

"Just in time," I heard Harper behind me as he grabbed my hand and led me to the dance floor.

"Where have you been?" I asked.

"I had to take care of some business that couldn't wait," Harper answered. "Promise I'll explain later. Sorry I'm so late, babycakes, but I'm here now."

Harper put his arms around me and we began to dance. The song was so slow that we didn't spend much time separated. It was a walkers' song, but I had only recently learned the very basics of walking, so we pretty much had an old-fashioned slow dance.

Even though the contest was still a few days away, I felt as though every move we made was already being evaluated and judged. Depending on the direction Harper turned me, I was able to catch a few glimpses of smiles, a few frowns, and even a pair of twisted lips. Typical. As nice as it was to be in his arms, I couldn't get this "business" of his off my mind.

The song ended and the music picked up the pace again. Harper walked me back to our table.

"May I have this dance?" said a voice I didn't recognize.

I turned with a smile only to realize that it was none other than Kurt "Kryptonite" Curtis extending his hand for a dance.

Holy shit! I thought. I was sure that I had become as pale as a ghost.

"C'mon," Krytonite continued, "I've seen you out there. Let's go to work, stepper!"

"You got that, Ginger," Harper winked and grabbed Sasha's hand for a dance.

As I headed to the dance floor with Kurt, he was already twirling his way to land on the spot he wanted.

Oh my goodness, what am I gonna do? I thought, beside myself with worry. I was mentally preparing myself for utter embarrassment when I suddenly remembered something Cam had said to me in one of our practices:

"Gigi, you are a natural dancer. Just feel the music and stay on your count. Don't worry about *his* count. It is *his* job to keep up with you, not the other way around."

Okay, let me give that a shot. It started out easy. I caught all of Kurt's turns and signals and was beginning to feel more confident.

All of a sudden, he released my hands and started spinning. I thought he was going to drill himself into the ground when he stopped cold in his tracks and started some other kind of unrecognizable, penguin-like footwork. Soon he was off spinning again and he pulled me into his tornado so that I was spinning with him. Thankfully it was only for a few rotations, although it felt like I was moving at the speed of light, and then we landed back on the earth and resumed the eight count until the song was over.

"That was nice," Kurt said. "What's your name, stepper?"

"I'm Gigi," I said, almost out of breath.

"Oh yeah, Harp's new partner," Kurt recalled. "I enjoyed the dance. He's doing a nice job with you. Good luck tomorrow, and I will catch up to you for round two."

All I could do was politely smile. I could find absolutely no words that would suffice as a reply to that statement.

"Girl, you did that!" Vivian cheered.

"Oh my goodness, Viv," I said. "Can you believe that craziness?"

"Kurt doesn't just ask anybody to dance, so he's been watching you," Vivian concluded.

"Why do you always have something extra to say about folks?" I asked. "It was only a dance, and I am glad that it is over. I was terrified out there!"

"You looked good, honey," Vivian said with a laugh. "I've been stepping almost three years, and I am still nervous dancing with Kurt. You just go with it and let him do his thing."

"There is really no other choice," I agreed.

After that exercise in terror, I was more than happy to have the opportunity to sit back down at the table. As I pulled out my fan, I took a minute to look around the room.

Both Sasha and Harper were on the dance floor. Greg had come and gone. I saw Stacey in a corner having a conversation with CJ, and Cam was talking to one of the out-of-town workshop instructors. The twins had gotten a good turnout for the beginning of this year's weekend of events. The mood of the room was pleasant and uncomplicated. I realized now I was more than a woman trying to learn this dance. I had actually become a part of these surroundings that were so new to me just one year ago.

∽

Sasha had driven us both to the set, and when it ended, she was fine with Harper taking me home. Besides, she was having a conversation with Zachary, the photographer we had met at the holiday set a few months ago. Turned out he had been filling in for Dolly on the night he first snapped our picture.

"What kept you tonight? Did you close your sale on the townhome?" I asked Harper on the ride home. I couldn't stop wondering what made him almost two hours late.

"I did, Ginger," Harper answered, "but that is not what kept me. As I was leaving the appointment with my buyers, I got a call from my dance partner from two years ago. She is in town and wanted to see if we could get together."

Silence.

"I told you about her once before," Harper said. "Her name is Alex. We were tight, not dating or anything, but we were close. Remember I mentioned her to you—at this time last year? She moved to California and has been dating some dude who is also her new dance partner."

"Okay," I said.

"Since you aren't going to ask, the answer is no, I didn't meet her anywhere. We just talked," Harper continued.

"Okay," I repeated.

"Ginger, look at me," he demanded.

I turned my head to look at him as he drove. The look on my face must have spoken volumes.

"Nothing is going on," Harper reassured. "We haven't spoken in over a year, so we were just catching up on family, friends, and the circle. She told me about LA and how different the vibe is there, but the same mess happens even all the way out in the west."

"Okay," I said again as I turned my head back to face the windshield.

"And of course I told her that I have a new dance partner, who also happens to be my girlfriend," Harper said.

"You told her that?" I asked.

"Why wouldn't I tell her that?" Harper answered. "It's the truth, right?"

I finally smiled and nodded.

"She's dramatic, but she's cool, Ginger," Harper continued. "If we run into her tomorrow, I will introduce you. She had a ton of questions about you, but I told her she would have to meet you for herself."

Yeah, I just bet she did.

"Cool," I said, trying not to overreact, "but I am already nervous about the contest. I don't need to have to fight any ex-girlfriends on top of everything else."

"You aren't joking either, are you?" Harper asked.

"Nope," I answered.

"Two things wrong with that statement: first she was *not* my girlfriend, and second, if there's gonna be a girl fight, I need front row."

"Very funny, Harper," I said with a sneer. "If she wanted to see you so badly, why didn't she just come to the set tonight?"

"She said she was tired from the trip," Harper explained.

"But somehow she had enough energy to meet you someplace else, huh?" I asked.

"Relax, Ginger," Harper said. "You must know by now that I am exactly where I want to be. When I told you tonight that I had to take care of something that couldn't wait, that is precisely what I was doing. I am not as naïve as you might think when it comes to women, Ginger. But you have to trust me to handle some things on my own. Like I said, we were close, *past* tense. And besides that, it was over two years ago. I told her that once she saw you, she would know why I was falling head over heels for you."

"You are such a charmer, Mr. Drake," I answered with a smile.

"It's easy to be charming when you're telling the truth," Harper said. "I know that we still have a lot to learn about each other, and every new situation is a test. All I ask is for you to give me the benefit of the doubt and believe me when I tell you that I am cool with you and me."

I believed him. I really wanted to believe him. He had

given me absolutely no reason not to believe him. Even still, it was hard to shake all the madness that had fallen upon my ears over the last few months. The complicated relationship between Stacey and CJ. The story Harper told me about Link and his talent for alienating women. Harper himself admitting to being overly "friendly" to more than one woman at a time. I was really starting to fall for this guy—I just didn't want to be a casualty.

∽

Day two of the big contest weekend. After a day full of workshops being instructed by visiting steppers, it was time for the evening's event, *Steppin' for a Cause.* Everyone was to wear jeans and their favorite steppers T-shirt and bring canned goods to be donated in lieu of purchasing a ticket for the set. Steppers were always organizing fund-raising events for worthy causes. Steppers were advocates for the prevention of all types of cancer, diabetes, and other terminal illnesses, along with community outreach like college fairs and job placement workshops.

The room was packed. This night, I arrived to the set with Harper, and Sasha was planning to meet me a little later. Harper and I had decided to reserve a room at the host hotel for the next two nights to make contest logistics a little easier and because we would be in and out of the hotel all weekend long.

As usual, Harper and I hit the dance floor as soon as we entered the room. I noticed DJ Donnie again at the DJ stand

and the music was on fire. We had three great dances before I finally took a seat. After about an hour, Sasha arrived. We sat and talked while Harper made his way around the room, decisively dancing with the out-of-town guests as CJ and Cam had always instructed the Untouchable Steppers men to do. Soon there was a break in the music and CJ took the stage.

"Again, welcome to the second night of our grand three-day steppers' weekend. I would like to welcome Ryan Rich of Foods from the Heartland to the stage. Give him a steppers' round of applause."

The crowd cheered as Mr. Rich explained the purpose and mission of his organization and how much he appreciated fellow organizations like Untouchable Steppers for donating to such a worthy cause. It was touching to hear how much impact could be had through the donations provided by events like this. The human spririt was alive and kicking in the room tonight.

Everyone was basking in the glow of charitable feelings from having done a good deed for the evening when the music started again. It was close to midnight now, and I was about ready to go. DJ Donnie played a slow one and Harper grabbed my hand.

"Last dance," he said.

"Okay," I said.

We had such a nice, close, and romantic dance. Harper held me tight, whispering things in my ear to make me giggle like a schoolgirl. I knew what was about to happen in that hotel room. I couldn't wait for that song to end.

Finally, I thought to myself as Harper kissed me at the end of the song, took my hand, and we headed for the door.

"Oops!" I said. "Left my fan on the table! And let me run and give Sasha a hug good night."

I dropped Harper's hand and headed back to the table where Sasha and I had been sitting.

"Harper Drake!" I turned around just in time to see a woman flail her arms around my boyfriend's neck and kiss him on the mouth.

"What the hell?" Harper said as he pushed the woman back. "Alex?"

"Hey, boo, it's been too long," the woman slurred.

"Alex, what are you doing? Take your drunk ass somewhere and sit down." Harper was angry now, but motioning for my hand.

"C'mon, you know no one can do it like me and you on that dance floor," Alex said. "Besides, she's barely been dancing for a year, Harp."

This bitch was talking to him like I wasn't even standing there.

"Why don't you let me worry about that," Harper replied. "C'mon, Ginger."

We had less than twenty-four hours before the start of the contest and I was a wreck. Harper took me firmly by the hand and led me to the elevators. I didn't even want him to touch me. He barely got the door to our hotel room open before I started in on him.

"Just friends, huh? Stop bullshitting me, Harper. You will not make a fool of me in front of all these people!" I yelled.

"Calm down," Harper said.

"This is how you *handled* things with her?" I asked. "She apparently did not get the right message. I told you I was not going to be in the middle of this mess. I should have listened to Vivian all along. I am done. I am not doing this."

I grabbed my empty overnight bag and started packing.

"What are you doing, Ginger?" Harper asked.

"What does it look like, genius?" I replied.

"Looks like you're running," Harper said.

"Well, what does it matter?" I asked. "You obviously won't have any problems replacing me as your partner for tomorrow. *Alex* looks like she will be happy to oblige you in more ways than one."

"Would you just stop a minute and sit your ass down," Harper started. "Please."

I sat on the bed.

"Listen. I did not lie to you. I told you I had a past in this circle, and she is part of it," he said.

"But you said you told her about us last night? That means that shit was deliberate," I concluded.

"Of course, but she was also drunk as a skunk," Harper explained to absolutely no avail.

"Drunk or not, like Vivian says, sometimes bitches just need to be treated like bitches. If you can't handle this, I will," I said with conviction.

"I got this, Ginger," Harper said. "No excuses for what happened, but I will handle it. You are the woman I want to be with, so unpack that bag because you are exactly where you are supposed to be."

Just as I was about to let Harper put his arms around me, his phone beeped with a text message.

"It's her, isn't it?" I asked.

"Yep," Harper answered, "and I'm glad it is so we can be done with this right now."

Harper held his phone so that I could see the message which read: *Whatcha doin?*

Harper replied: *Call me.*

His phone rang almost instantly, and he answered it using his speaker so that I could listen.

"I knew you missed me, boo," Alex said.

"Alex, you know I ain't never been your boo," Harper replied.

"Whatever, Harp. I'm in room 631 and the door is wide open," the tramp said.

"Well, Alex, I am in room 729 with my girl, and we are about to go bed, so you should probably lock that door," Harper answered.

"Your loss, Harp." Alex hung up the phone abruptly. No doubt to reach out to the next number on her booty call list.

"Are you satisfied now?"

"I guess so, Harper," I answered, "until she does it again."

"That ain't happening," Harper said.

"How long were you two together?" I asked.

"That's just it," Harper started. "We were never really together, not in the sense that you mean. We were dance partners, and because of that we spent a lot of time together. Stuff got heated a few times and that was that. When I told you I learned the hard way—she was a part of that whole mess before she left town. As I am sure you noticed, the word *discretion* is not in her vocabulary. But I still take responsibility for my part in that situation. She is a part of my past. Period."

I was quiet, and I'm sure my bottom lip was poked out, but I had to give him credit for proving to me that he was telling the truth right there on the spot like that. Not many guys would have taken the chance of putting their past on blast. Certainly not the ones I had been involved with. Harper was beginning to show me a level of respect that I hadn't ever received from any male, aside from my father, up to this point in my life.

"Now bring your angry sexy ass over here. I don't want any bullshit to come between us," Harper said, "especially not that kind of bullshit."

Harper kissed me on the forehead and hugged me tightly. He lay down behind me on the bed with his arm around my waist, holding my hand.

"I'm sorry that happened, Ginger," he whispered in my ear. "I don't ever want you to feel uncomfortable or disrespected because of me."

I didn't say a word. I let Harper continue to hold me like that all night long. I don't think either of us got any sleep at all.

∾ *Chapter Twenty-One*

The next morning Harper was already gone when I opened my eyes. I could hear a light spring rain outside of the hotel window and could still smell Harper on the sheets. As I rolled over to check the time, I found the note he left on the bedside table:

Showing @ 9 a.m. . . . see you later, babycakes.

Harper had already told me he was working in the morning, but the note was a nice touch. I sat up in bed, still wearing my clothes from the night before. Naturally, I was unable to completely shake the events that had taken place over the last twenty-four hours, but I had decided to trust Harper and give him the benefit of the doubt. And besides that, there was too much going on today to put any more energy into madness.

The day of the contest flew by. I spent most of my morning with Grace and Isabel and then made my way back to the hotel. I attended two workshops and was able to spend quite a bit of time speaking with several out-of-town instructors and their students. Ant and his group of Milwaukee steppers were in town, so it was nice to see them again. Vivian and Stacey were pulling together contest details, so Sasha and I took a little break and headed to the nearby mall for a little shopping. Before I knew it, the contest was just a few short hours away.

Harper had made it to the hotel around dinnertime, so we decided to order room service. I added two vodka tonics to the order to help me relax and calm my nerves. Then it was time to get ready. Earlier that day, Grace picked out my shoes and accessories and had given her final stamp of approval on our red and white outfits for the contest. Isabel, on the other hand, had given me the biggest hug of encouragement that a thirteen-year-old could give. Since the girls were home and we were at the hotel, I called them on FaceTime so they could see us before the contest began.

"Me and your mom are ready to win some money!" Harper said with a big smile.

"Mom looks nervous," Grace chimed in.

"Oh yeah?" Harper asked.

"A little, but I'm okay," I said.

"Well, you certainly look the part," Harper added. "You look beautiful in red, Ginger."

"Told you Mom would look beautiful, Grace," Isabel interrupted.

"All right, you two," I said before Grace had a chance to make a comeback. "Like I told you this morning, in bed by eleven thirty. Heidi will be there to check on you guys again around bedtime."

"Good luck, Mom!" my girls shouted as we were saying goodnight. "You too, Harper!"

We said goodnight to the girls as we ended our video call.

"You ready?" Harper asked as he put my arm in his.

"Ready as I'm gonna get," I answered.

Harper shut the door behind us and we headed to the ballroom.

∽

The scenery at the contest set was not unlike that of a year ago. The main difference was the color theme for this year was blue instead of last year's purple. When we arrived, the line dancers were already on the floor doing their thing.

"You guys look great!" It was Dolly snapping our picture.

"Thanks," I said, smiling for the camera and watching for that crazy woman in my peripheral vision.

"Wow, you two make the perfect couple." It was Cam patting Harper on the back.

"What's up, Cam?" Harper said, shaking Cam's hand.

"You two ready?" Cam asked. "Just stay calm, feel the music, and remember everything *I* taught you, Gigi."

We all laughed as Cam tried to lighten the mood.

"Thanks, Cam," I said. "I am going out there to have some fun and do what my partner tells me to do."

"That's what's up!" Cam said with a grin. "Y'all are gonna be all right."

Cam headed back to the front of the room as Harper and I started in the direction of the contestant seating area.

"Here's your fan, honey!" Sasha said. "You guys look like winners for sure!"

"Thanks, Sasha," I answered, giving her a big hug. "I got a little distracted last night, so thanks for grabbing my fan. Have you seen Stacey or Vivian?"

"Girl, you know they are running around dealing with last-minute details like always," Sasha replied.

Harper had walked away as I was speaking with Sasha.

After a few minutes, I was again on my way to join him and sit with the rest of the contest participants. Instead, I turned to see Alex talking to Harper—again. She looked in my direction and motioned for me to join them. I was headed toward the two of them when I was intercepted by Kurt Kryptonite himself.

"Hey, Gigi," Kurt started, "I wanted to tell you again that I enjoyed our dance last night."

"Thanks, Kurt," I said, looking over his shoulder at Harper and Alex.

"I also wanted to extend a personal invitation to join the charter members of Kryptonite, Ltd," Kurt explained.

"What?" I asked.

"For only three thousand dollars, you can become a part of my elite group of steppers as a 'member-at-large.' Your membership buys your admission to all my classes and workshops four times per year on my quarterly visits to your city, and four additional times a year if or when you are in Chicago or any other city where I am teaching. Best thing about it, you are able to use my name for marketing purposes to increase attendance when—"

"What?" I repeated, stopping Kurt midsentence.

"We can set up a payment plan if you need one, Gigi," Kurt explained further.

"Totally flattered, Kurt," I lied. "Catch me after the contest."

"Cool," Kurt said. "Good luck, sweetheart."

I walked past Kurt and promptly took my place beside Harper, who was still facing Alex.

"Gigi, I was just telling Harp here that I am really sorry about last night," Alex said. "I had too much to drink and I was way out of line."

"It's all good," Harper said. "Let's go get our seats, babycakes."

Harper was obviously trying to be dismissive and move on from the conversation. He pulled at my hand.

"Harper is a great guy," Alex continued. "And you seem nice too. You two look good together."

"Thanks," I said with a glare, as I started to walk away with Harper.

"Go ahead, honeybun. I need to make one more stop at the little girls' room," I said as I dropped Harper's hand. "That vodka is catching up to me. I'll be right there."

Harper continued on to claim our seats as I walked back toward Alex.

"It's Alex, right?" I asked.

"Yes. Again, good luck tonight," she said, smiling perhaps genuinely.

"Thanks. But let me just be perfectly clear," I said with my best smile ever. "Don't let the high heels and the pretty smile fool you. If you have the audacity to put your lips on him again, I will *fuck you up*."

I smiled again and walked away.

I felt a hand on my shoulder a few moments later. As I clenched my fist, ready to strike, I turned around to see Vivian's smile.

"What did you say to that girl?" Vivian asked. She could tell that I was on the verge of exploding. "Her face is all red!"

"You know how you say it, Viv," I answered her with a certain look on my face.

"Oh shit, you had to treat a bitch like a bitch, G?" Vivian was laughing so hard she had her hands on her knees.

"You know it," I answered. "Now let me go catch up with my man."

"Good luck, girl," Vivian said as I walked away, still laughing.

❦

CJ and Cam cleared the dance floor and announced that the start of the contest would begin in about the next hour. Harper had drawn the number two, so we would be in the second round of couples to take the floor. At least I would get it over with early.

"Welcome back, everyone!" Cam started. "We are so happy to see so many familiar faces back to join us for this year's US vs. Them Steppers' Contest brought to you by none other than Untouchable Steppers!"

The crowd cheered. CJ then took the stage and introduced the contest judges. In that instant, my nerves came crashing down out of nowhere. I was sitting in a total daze. My eyes looked on as the judges took the floor and performed their own stepping demonstration. Next, as in years past, Ivy was out on the floor with her Dynamic Divas of Dance to put on yet another stellar line dance performance with her crew. Even that didn't put me at ease. I expected that I would be a little nervous, but this was too much. At one point during all of the pre-contest activity, I actually felt as if I was having an out-of-body experience. I was seeing the dancers and hearing the music, but it was as if I weren't actually present.

"You okay?" Harper leaned over and whispered in my ear.

"I think so," I whispered back.

Harper squeezed my hand. I knew that was his way of telling me it was going to be okay.

Suddenly those house lights were up and judgment filled the air. I was paralyzed.

"All right, time for the main event!" Cam was back on-stage. "For the first time, we are going to do something a little different this year. Our first two couples coming to the floor will be last year's winners. Let's hear it for Rocco and Lena representing Minnesota, and Kurt and Janet, last year's first place out-of-town winners! DJ, start spinnin' those ones and twos for us. Let's go to work, steppers!"

The crowd was on its feet as the couples started to dance. I looked at Harper like a deer in headlights. How in the hell were we supposed to follow these two winning couples from last year? I remembered how everyone basically offered obligatory applause to the couple who took the floor after Kurt out of sheer diplomacy because no one was watching them. This was definitely the worst-case scenario. My heart was beating out of my chest.

"We will be fine." Harper was in my ear again.

I watched Kurt and Janet in their solid black outfits take the floor by storm in their usual course. Unlike last year, I didn't hear the chant of "Kryptonite! Kryptonite!" rising from the Chicago tables in that city's section of the room. Rocco and Lena were as fabulous as always. They wore a stunning royal blue this year and made their way around the perimeter of the dance floor as if they owned the place.

Both of their performances were spectacular. Absolutely flawless in their combinations and connecting turns. And then Kurt did the unthinkable. He went spiraling out of control, hooked Lena around the waist, whirling her into a carousel turn, only to spin her back out to her partner. Lena was visibly shaken, but Rocco quickly eased the tension with a close-in walking move to quickly regain control of his part- ner. Their recovery was seamless, at least to a beginner's eyes. As I listened to the cheers, I couldn't tell if the crowd was booing or cheering at this inconceivable exhibition in foolishness. Like the champions they are, Rocco and Lena finished their dance with style, grace, and beauty. When the song ended, words were quietly exchanged as Rocco was obviously angry with Kurt for interrupting his and Lena's performance.

"Let's give it up for last year's winners!" Cam said as the crowd applauded the performances. "My man, Kryptonite, is always good for the unexpected," Cam continued in his effort to gloss over Kurt's crazy antics.

This is just great, I thought. As if his regular dance weren't enough of a distraction, Kurt had to go all out and act like a total clown.

"Coming to the floor next . . . ooh, we got a local newbie coming out, ya'll!" Cam said with a big smile. "Let's hear it for couple number twenty-five, Tom and Bobbie from

Mil-town, and reppin' Minnesota for the first time, couple number thirty-one, Harper and Gigi!"

We stood from our chairs as the crowd applauded. I was sure Harper could hear my heart beating out of my chest as he took my hand and led me to the dance floor.

My feet felt as if they were the weight of cement blocks. When Harper finally managed to drag me to our spot on the floor, my terror only increased. It may have been my imagination, but I could've sworn I was hearing voices:

"She's only been dancing a year. What is she gonna do out there?"

"You know he only picked her because they are sleeping together."

"Have you seen her dance? She has absolutely no footwork at all."

Ordinarily, such spiteful jeering would simply motivate me to prove everyone wrong. But at this moment, I was frozen. I suddenly remembered that a few of last years' couples complained about never hearing their personal music selection on the dance floor. Harper and I had practiced to the same song over and over, so I was hoping that the DJ was on point. We stood in that corner of the floor opposite the couple from Milwaukee for what seemed to be an hour. The music started and I was at least relieved that I recognized the fact that it was our song.

Harper looked me in the eye, put his arm around my waist tightly, and said, "It's just you and me out here, Ginger."

Now what? The dance started, that's what. My feet didn't remember the eight-count pattern. I had danced to this song a hundred times and my feet wouldn't fall in line. We didn't have a routine, but we had practiced enough to know that there were certain moves that we wanted to show the judges. I was screwing up.

Then Harper pulled me close. He didn't say a word and he didn't look angry. He smiled and we moved in a slow circle for a few counts of eight. Then I felt the dip coming.

"No, not here, not yet!" I whispered in Harper's ear.

"Relax," he whispered back.

Harper dipped me all the way to the floor and topped it off with a kiss. The crowd went wild.

Then something happened. When I was back in an upright position, my feet started to remember what to do. We began our dance again and made our way around the perimeter of the floor exchanging playful smiles and romantic glances as if we had been partners forever. I was catching all of Harper's signals for fancy turns and synchronized footwork patterns as if I could feel them coming before he gave them to me. Then I realized that I was actually having a good time. More than that, I realized I was safely in the arms of a wonderful partner—on and off the dance floor.

Our smiles must have been contagious because the audience was smiling and cheering right along with us. Then it was over. Harper was right, that was the fastest four minutes of my life.

When we left the dance floor, the couples headed back to their seats. There were three more performances before the first round of winners was announced. I couldn't do it. I was out of there.

Much like I had behaved with Harper the night of our very first dance over a year ago, I left him and headed for the ladies room in the hall.

I was sure that I was about to have a heart attack when Sasha opened the ladies room door.

"You guys were great!" Sasha squealed.

"Really?" I asked.

"Yes, it was so cute! You two looked like you were born to dance with one another."

"Thanks," I replied with a shallow breath.

"Are you okay, Gigi?" Sasha asked. "You are so pale!"

"I don't know." I said. "I couldn't believe how nervous I was. I totally screwed up at the beginning of the dance."

"No one noticed that!" Sasha said. "People were smiling right along with you guys because you were fun to watch."

"Really?" I asked again. "I have to admit, it was so much fun being in Harper's arms in front of that crowd. You don't think he was disappointed, do you?"

"I'm telling you," Sasha continued, "you two were wonderful. The beaming smile on Harper's face as you two walked off the floor had no resemblance to disappointment. And what did I tell you yesterday? This is not your whole life; this is supposed to be *fun*! You better pull yourself together, though, because I have a feeling that you are about to do it all over again. The final round is in a few minutes."

"No way!" I said. "Rocco and Lena will win again. Aside from that garbage Kurt pulled, they were flawless as usual."

"I don't know if someone else snatching your dance partner away from you counts as flawless, but hey, I'm a newbie to this thing. Let's get back out there and see the rest of the competition."

"You go ahead, Sasha. I still need a minute."

After Sasha left the ladies room, I took a seat on a small stool next to the mirror. I looked at myself in this red twirly dress with matching red high heels and couldn't believe what I had just done. I was taken back to my days as a ballerina. Even though I had been on display in dance recitals for years, it was not the same. Not only were ballet routines entirely memorized and rehearsed again and again, but the audiences were much kinder back in the old days. People didn't jeer and frown at little girls wearing fluffy tutus.

I stood up and dusted myself off. I decided it was time to test out my newfound courage and get back out there to support my dance partner. But not before I stopped at the bar.

By the time I threw back my second vodka tonic, the last two couples were halfway through their routines. I waited by the door so as not to disturb anyone mid-twirl. Harper looked my way with an expression on his face as if to say, "Where the hell have you been?"

I waved to him with drink in hand, and he nodded and smiled.

I was still a little shocked that I had just competed in my first stepping contest. Win or lose, I had gained a new confidence in myself that was glowing all around me like a halo. Maybe some of the jeering and mocking wasn't all wrong, but it didn't matter. I was happy. I was having fun. I was falling in love with Harper. And, if I was being honest with myself, I was falling in love with stepping, too.